A Hanging in Sweetwater

A Hanging in Sweetwater

Stephen
Overholser

Thorndike Press • Chivers Press
Thorndike, Maine USA   Bath, England

This Large Print edition is published by Thorndike Press, USA and by Chivers Press, England.

Published in 1999 in the U.S. by arrangement with Golden West Literary Agency.

Published in 1999 in the U.K. by arrangement with Golden West Literary Agency.

U.S. Hardcover 0-7862-2206-9 (Western Series Edition)
U.K. Hardcover 0-7540-3979-X (Chivers Large Print)
U.K. Softcover 0-7540-3980-3 (Camden Large Print)

Thorndike Large Print ® Western Series.

The tree indicium is a trademark of Thorndike Press.

The text of this Large Print edition is unabridged.
Other aspects of the book may vary from the original edition.

Set in 16 pt. Plantin.

Printed in the United States on permanent paper.

British Library Cataloguing-in-Publication Data available

Library of Congress Cataloging-in-Publication Data

Overholser, Stephen.
    A hanging in Sweetwater / Stephen Overholser.
      p. cm.
    ISBN 0-7862-2206-9 (lg. print : hc : alk. paper)
    1. Large type books. I. Title.
  [PS3565.V43H36   1999]
  813´.54—dc21   99-41164

To my father

CHAPTER I

As a boy I remember hearing a preacher say a man's life runs in a big circle, a circle of years, and at the end — which is also the beginning — a man reaches salvation if he's led a good and true life. I never gave that idea much thought, except to wonder exactly what a good and true life was, and what it felt like to be a man, until the year I ran away from home and saw the end of my own circle coming fast.

It happened this way: I heard one hell of an ear-busting explosion, smelled powder smoke in the air, then felt water flooding over my face. I blinked and choked and when my eyes cleared I saw an old Indian looking down at me, his dark angry face set against the blue sky.

Water. You take it for granted until the time comes when you don't have any — at least you do if you're as green as I was. I had gone two full days without water, and only a swallow the day before. I was dry as dead wood and dizzy all the time.

My mare, Pepper, was taking it hard,

7

too. Her head drooped and she was making a sound that had me scared. It was a moaning, wheezing sound, an animal sound I'd never heard before. I was afraid it was a dying sound.

The air was purely cold in that high desert out in the middle of Wyoming. The wind was so steady that it seemed like it had been blowing forever. My skin was parched dry and burned just as if I had been out in the sun and heat.

Two days ago I got fooled into leaving the main road. I had come to an unmarked fork and took the one that turned out to be nothing but a ranch road. After half a day of riding I saw I'd made a mistake.

I topped a low hill and reined up in surprise. That windswept hill overlooked the fanciest ranch I'd ever seen. It was the kind I'd read about in library books back home, but never really thought I'd see. The ranch was set in the middle of a grassy basin among leafy cottonwood trees, nothing like the desolate sagebrush country I'd been riding in. The main house and even the outbuildings were painted pure white, white as a bed sheet. The road I was on ran through the basin to the ranch house and stopped there.

Of all the things I could have done, I

picked the worst. I skirted that ranch and started out across country, heading west, the same direction I'd gone since the day I left home. But I had no sense of Wyoming distance. I didn't know the territory of Wyoming had counties bigger than the whole state of Massachusetts. I believed if I kept riding west I would come to a town or another ranch or at least a road of some kind. Turning around to get back on the main road seemed like an awful waste of time.

I didn't even have brains enough to ride into the ranch to ask for directions. I could have asked for a job, too. For I saw myself becoming a top-rated cowboy as well as a man. I knew something was going to happen to me to make me a man. I didn't know what. I only knew it would happen. It was something I felt down deep inside me. And I believed it was coming soon for I was getting some years on me. I was almost sixteen.

The shimmering white buildings of that ranch down in the basin looked too good and fancy for a beginner like me. I figured I ought to go some place else, to a smaller outfit, to get some experience. Then I could ride into a big ranch like that white one without any scared feelings.

The water I carried lasted less than a day. I gave Pepper most of it, saving a swallow for myself. On the second day I kept riding west, still not seeing the trouble I was getting into. Often I saw small herds of antelope standing off in the distance. Sometimes they flashed their white tails and ran off; other times they would watch me curiously.

There was only one good thing about my little ride into the desert. If my father had sent any detectives after me, I lost them that day. Nobody but an Indian or a man with a water wagon in tow would have tried to cross that wind-blown desert like I did.

Spring 1889, that was. Or it would have been spring any place else. But the desert was high in that country, the winters long and harsh. The relentless wind had a bite to it, and seemed to get worse the farther west I rode. Either that, or I was weakening.

Riding through Nebraska a couple of weeks before I had seen drifts of snow in shallow gullies and on shady sides of hills. But not here. The wind must have blown it all away.

The farther west I rode, the more desolate the country became. The sagebrush became sparse and stunted. Nothing else grew but spindly little weeds and my own misery. I didn't see any more antelope. I didn't even see a bird that last day and a half.

I got to riding in rocky gully bottoms, hoping to find a pool of water or a patch of snow. But that was hard work for Pepper. The rocks she had to pick her way through were as big as melons. And by day's end she was walking slowly and I was hanging over her neck, trying to get out of the wind. Those rounded rocks began to look like bleached-out human skulls.

That night I made the driest dry camp I've ever made. I shivered in the starry, windy darkness. The wind cut through my blankets like knives. I don't think I slept for more than a few minutes at a time. Pepper kept knocking her hoofs against the rocks. Sometime during the night she started making that sound, a moan that came from deep inside her, rumbling and painful-sounding.

In the gray light of early morning I awoke with my eyes full of grit and tears and the taste of blood in my mouth. When I wiped the back of my hand across my lips, it came away red with blood and scabs.

The only food I had was what was left of some jerky I'd bought from a black I met while crossing the Mississippi on a ferry. He told me it was good meat and a little of it would keep me alive out there in the West where there weren't many stores. I started for I hadn't told the black man where I was going. Somehow in talking to me or looking at me he had guessed. I wondered if he had guessed I was a runaway, too.

But the jerky tasted like pure salt that morning. I couldn't get any of it down. All I could think about was a long swallow of water.

I had never been so tired. The wind was beating me to death. My head felt like it would spin off my neck. Every time I moved, pain shot through me. But I knew I had to saddle up Pepper and ride on. If I stayed I would die there.

I rode hunched over Pepper's neck as she plodded along the gully bottom, her shoes ringing against the rocks. I couldn't keep my eyes open for long. And when I did force them open, I couldn't see much. Everything was blurred with tears.

Over the wheezing sound Pepper was making, and over the roar of the desert wind, I began hearing another sound — or

I felt it. The sound was close, like a fly buzzing in my ear. But it wasn't a fly. When I recognized the sound, I wished I hadn't. For it was the laughter of my father. Back home he always laughed at me when I'd done something foolish.

Pepper missed a step and I jerked awake. Her head was nearly dragging on the rocks, she was so worn down. But Pepper wasn't a horse that would quit. She'd go and go. That walk of hers had carried me halfway across these United States without a complaint. Wherever I wanted to go, she went. It was as though she knew I was out on my own now, and it was up to her to take care of me.

Then I heard my father laughing at me again, his faraway voice telling me I was a left-handed fool who had never done anything right and never would. In my mind I wanted to yell back at him: *You wait until I get out West. I won't make any more mistakes and everything will be all right. I'll find my place.*

I slowly tumbled into a dark cold pit. It was mighty deep, probably the deepest on earth. I fell forever. I heard nothing but the sound of the wind and felt nothing but its chill. It was scary to fall like that, but at the same time I knew something good was

13

going to happen. I knew that when I struck the pit's bottom, I would be away from my father, I would be a man, and all my questions would be answered. For that was the end of the circle. And for me it was the beginning.

The explosion was loud and so close it set my ears to ringing. My nose filled with powder smoke. I was still falling through space, but now I was confused and knew something was wrong. Then I hit the bottom of the pit with the purely terrible force of water hitting my face.

I choked and gasped for air. When I tried to see what was happening, bright sunlight burned my eyes. More water hit me, washing down my cheeks and lips. I got a taste of it. Water! Bringing my hand up to shield my eyes, I looked up and saw the scowling face of an Indian outlined by the sky.

I couldn't defend myself. I lay stretched out on the rocky bottom of the gully I'd been riding in. My sight wasn't true. I must have hit my head hard enough to knock myself cockeyed. There were four or five blurry Indians leaning over me, then I saw only one, then four or five again.

When my head cleared and the powerful ringing in my ears stopped, I saw that I was looking at one Indian. His mouth opened to show yellowed teeth. He grinned and made noises I couldn't understand. He helped me sit up and I caught his smell. It was a strange one, leathery and smoky, not a bad smell, but new to me and distinctive.

The purely sweetest drink of water I've ever had was the one that Indian gave me. When I ran out of breath and had to quit drinking, I looked at the canteen and saw U. S. ARMY stamped on its side. I took another look at the Indian. He wore a stained buckskin shirt, faded blue army trousers and tall moccasins.

The canteen fell from my hand. For suddenly I knew that he'd had to kill a soldier to get those trousers and the canteen.

I must have made a poor try at escaping. The Indian grabbed me right away and held me down. I was as weak as a cat. He made some more grumbling sounds and this time I got some sense out of them. He said he was a friend of the soldiers. He turned loose of me then as though to prove it. When I looked at him, he smiled at me, but I was still so scared I was shaking.

I didn't know what to do. I felt trapped in that gully like an animal in a cage. Finally I tried to look friendly toward the

Indian. His hair was plastered down and tied into twin braids. His dark eyes gleamed like oil. On his hip I saw a holstered hand gun that looked fifty years old. It was dirty and rusty, but I didn't doubt the thing worked.

Seeing that revolver made me remember I'd heard a gunshot. I started to add things up. I looked around and saw Pepper lying in the rocks a few feet away from me. Her brown eyes were open, but she wasn't seeing anything. Her cheek and mouth were shiny with blood.

I felt myself slipping back into that cold pit again, and when the Indian grumbled some low sounds and put his rough hand on the back of my neck, I went in all the way, falling through the darkness and through the wind.

CHAPTER II

I woke up flat on my back with a ceiling slowly turning overhead. Rough-cut beams supported small, crossways boards making a strange, moving pattern. I closed my eyes and might have slept for a while for when I opened them again, the ceiling was still. I raised up and saw I was lying on a hard rawhide bunk, covered by a heavy quilt. I caught the faint smell of wood smoke in the air. In the dim, gloomy light I saw the inside of a low one-room cabin built of logs.

"You're awake," I heard a woman say. "Stay right there. Don't you dare move."

When I looked toward the voice I saw a woman rise up out of the gloom like a ghost and silently cross the length of the cabin. I saw that the floor was dirt and that the woman wore moccasins. I thought I'd seen another pair like them, but couldn't remember where.

When the woman opened the door for light, I squinted my eyes. She stood before a wood stove and stirred something in a pan. I lay back again and closed my eyes until I heard her say, "You take this down. You have to get something in your stomach. When was the last time you had anything to eat? Come on, now, I know it smells bad, but it's good for you. You're skinny as string, do you know that?"

I watched her as she spoke. The skin of her face was smooth and creamy. One long braid of hair fell in front of her shoulder, the other behind. She was a fair-looking woman, of good form, though she appeared somehow tough, too. She wasn't hard or mean-looking, but sturdy and tough. The hand that held the spoon was dark and callused, fingernails broken, like a man's.

When the spoon passed under my nose on the way to my mouth, I jerked back. The stuff smelled rotten, like a dead varmint.

"Come on, now," the woman said sternly. "It's bad, but it ain't that damn bad. The smell is worse than the taste. This here is Indian tea and it's good for you. Cures your ails. Come on, now."

I took a breath, held it, and opened my mouth. I felt the cracks in my lips breaking open. Then the warm spoon was in my mouth and it was too late to change my mind. The woman had been right. It didn't taste as bad as it smelled. But how could it? It was the worst-smelling stuff in the world. I felt my stomach quiver, but the Indian tea stayed down. I wouldn't have been surprised if it had come right back up, all over that colorful quilt.

She fed me a few more spoonfuls and went on to tell me about all the lives that had been saved by Indian tea. She wasn't sure but what it had saved her life a few times when she'd been laid up with an ailment. Then she pointed to a little shelf on the log wall beside me.

"You see those bottles?" she asked.

I raised up higher, glad to be away from the Indian tea, and saw a shelf crowded with bottles. Some were tall and narrow, others were low and wide. They all had labels with various pictures and strange names. One that caught my eye showed a fat naked girl holding a leafy branch before her. Over her head were the words SYRUP OF FIGS. I guessed that was a fig branch in her hand.

"Those are patent medicines," the woman said. "I bought them from drummers. Some are good, but some of them ain't worth a . . . a cow chip. But Indian tea, it's good enough to guarantee. And I don't pay for it. I take a little sugar and swap it to White Wolf." She stopped talking and put her free hand on my forehead. "Why, look at you now. You've got some color in your face already. You're not so warm, either."

I felt sick to my stomach and feverish, but I nodded at her and tried to smile. I was afraid if I told her my true feelings, she would figure I needed more Indian tea.

"What's your name?" she asked. "Mine's Ella."

I didn't answer right off. During all those weeks of traveling I had been used to staying away from people, hoping no one would notice me. After I met the black man on the ferry and heard him make a close guess about me, I'd bought an oversized wool hat and worn it pulled low over my ears and just above my eyes. I thought if no one could see what I looked like, I'd be safe. I wore that hat for a week, then I lost it in a windstorm. But even when I was farther west I was afraid people were watching for me and trying to catch me so they could collect a reward. Boomer Hendricks gave me that idea. He was my best friend back home. Or I thought he was.

One day during recess Boomer Hendricks surprised me by saying he was planning to run away from home. He said he didn't know when exactly. He just knew he would one day. The reason I was surprised to hear him say it was that I couldn't see that he had anything to run away from. His father, a huge man who owned a livery, was gentle with horses and boys, and his mother was the best cook in our whole end of town. All the men said so in private when they gathered in the livery. Anybody who would run away from her was a pure fool.

But hearing Boomer say out loud that he would run away from home one day made me think about it more than I ever had before. I even started spending extra time in the school library to read books that told about the West and to study maps. I measured distances from one point to another, from one town to another. I looked for the best route to the West, but about the only thing I decided was that if we stayed on main roads and aimed west all the time, we would be in the West sooner or later. Once, while reading a book written by a Western explorer, I came across the line: "In the crisp and luxurious mornings we set out with the Sun to our backs; and after a restful noontime camp we rode across the prairie into the Sun."

We. For I always thought of Boomer being with me. We would ride away from the sun in the mornings and follow it in the afternoons. Though I'd never mentioned it to him, I couldn't imagine running away alone. But when I did tell him, he surprised me again.

"You're crazy," he said, staring at me like he had never seen me before. "You're crazy as a hoot owl."

At that moment, as we looked at each other, I not only knew he wouldn't go with me, I knew I didn't want him to.

"There's nothing crazy about it," I said. "One time you said you were going to run away."

"I never."

"You did, too. I heard you."

"Naw," Boomer said, "I probably said I was thinking about it. I'm not crazy enough to really do it."

We didn't walk to school together the next day or the day after. We avoided each other during recess. But then after school he caught up with me as I was on my way to my father's store.

"You still have that crazy idea about running away from home?" he asked, breathing hard.

I nodded.

Boomer caught his breath. "Don't do it. I've been thinking about you and about what you said. You'll get caught and your pa will give you a real whipping."

"I've had plenty of real ones," I said, "and I don't figure on waiting around for any more of them."

But Boomer's big head kept shaking like it was mounted on a spring. "Don't do it, don't do it. It's too dangerous. What are you going to do for money? How are you going to travel? On the train? That's how I'd do it, on the train."

Suddenly I realized that Boomer wanted to go with me, but he didn't have the nerve. I began to feel older than he, and wiser. "You'd get caught in a hurry. All they'd have to do is stop the train and you'd be caught like a bug in a can."

"Well, how are you going to do it?"

"I'm taking Pepper. She's mine."

"Pepper?" Boomer scoffed. "That plug will never make it. You're going to the West, aren't you? Don't you know how far away that is?"

Boomer didn't know that I'd been looking at maps since Christmas. And his idea of a good horse was a fast one. Pepper was probably the slowest horse in the county.

"You're crazier than a burned lizard," Boomer said. He picked up those sayings about hoot owls and burned lizards from the men who came to his father's livery.

"What are you going to do for money?" Boomer went on. "Your pa never gives you a nickel unless you're on your way to church."

"I've saved up enough," I said confidently. I had to lie to him. I was too ashamed to admit that I planned to steal money from my father. He kept about five hundred dollars in a strongbox beneath his bed. I knew where he kept the key. I figured I'd take two hundred. I thought of it as the pay I never got for all the hours I worked in his dry goods store. I knew I had the money coming to me, even more than two hundred at low wages, but I was still ashamed of having to steal it. I'd sat through too many sermons, I guessed.

"If your ma was alive, what would she say?" Boomer asked solemnly.

That wasn't a weapon he used very often. He knew he could usually clinch an argument by bringing up my mother. The truth was, if my mother had been alive, I probably wouldn't have been running away. My father had not been so cross and strict before she died.

"She doesn't have anything to worry about now," I said. "I have to look out for myself."

"Your pa is going to be mad," he said. "Real mad."

Boomer didn't know the half of it. When my father missed that two hundred dollars he would really blow up.

Boomer's eyes widened with a new idea. "You know what he'll do?"

He waited for me to guess, but as soon as I started to say something, he waved me quiet.

"Your pa will put up a big reward and pay it to anybody who finds you. He'll send out circulars with your picture on them. How are you going to get away from that?"

That was something I hadn't thought of, but I did my best to keep it from showing in my face. I would just have to be careful and stay clear of people.

"You know what else he might do?" Boomer asked. "He might hire detectives to go after you. Detectives can find anybody, you'd better believe that."

I believed it, all right. I thought I might become a detective myself if I ever got tired of being a cowboy. But that was something I'd already thought over and wasn't worried about. Detectives were expensive. My father would do just about anything to keep from spending money. Although when my mother died, I remembered, he put on the biggest funeral anybody in town could remember seeing. I didn't know what it cost, but it must have been near five or six hundred dollars. I had to admit that my father could spend money when he thought he had to.

"Are you still going?" Boomer asked.

I nodded. As we stood looking at each other, I had the feeling that he expected me to ask him to come with me. I wasn't about to now, but for a reckless moment I thought he was ready to say Yes — though it would have been No after he had a minute to think it over. But I didn't ask him. Our friendship had changed. I wasn't sure how, but it had. We couldn't back up.

"Well, when?" Boomer asked.

"Oh, not for a few weeks," I said, trying to make my voice sound easy. "I have a lot of things to do yet."

"You're really going."

I nodded.

A funny look was in Boomer's face now, like he was trying to watch me without my knowing it. He glanced away, then back at me again.

"Well," he said at last, looking at the ground, "see you tomorrow." He turned quickly, and walked away.

What I hadn't told Boomer was that I was ready to leave right then. Until then I had planned on waiting for school to be out late in the spring. But Boomer had helped me make up my mind. School didn't matter now. Nothing mattered. For I suddenly had the idea that Boomer planned to tell someone of my plans.

I ran straight home instead of going to the store. I took two hundred dollars from the strongbox, carefully putting the key back in the dresser drawer where it belonged. It might be several days after I was gone before my father discovered the missing money. The longer I could postpone that, the better.

For a minute I had a wild idea. It would be a good trick if I took the key with me. I remembered the salesman had bragged at length that the strongbox was guaranteed burglarproof, fireproof, and earthquakeproof. If I took the key with me, my father would find out the hard way if the guarantee was any good. It gave me pleasure to think of his rage at this trick, but I soon thought better of it. It would only give him more reason to hunt me down.

During school days I had to work four hours a day in the store. When I came in late that day I gave staying after school as my excuse. I had been telling quite a few lies in the last couple of hours, and I figured another wouldn't do me any more harm.

I remember that my father was in a good enough mood that he didn't bother to take a swat at me for coming in late. He told me to quit mumbling about school and to head straight for the stock room. A shipment of canned goods had come in that afternoon. I would have to uncrate the shipment, count each can and record the count, and then stock the shelves.

With no more than a glance my way, my father tossed an apron at me and said, "Do it right-handed for once."

That was his way of telling me not to make any mistakes. It seemed like I was always doing something wrong in the store. When I was careful he said I was working too slow. When I worked fast, I made mistakes. The harder I tried to do things right, the more mistakes I made.

But that afternoon in my father's store was my last one. That night, at midnight, I took Pepper and rode out, heading west.

★ ★ ★

I said to Ella, "My name's Boomer." I thought a minute, then said, "Boomer Jones."

"That's an uncommon name, Boomer. Boomer." She said it again, seeing how it fit her mouth, I guessed.

"Jones is pretty common," I said. "Back home, anyway."

Ella laughed. "Oh, you'll find plenty of Joneses out here, too. Smiths and Joneses behind every other bush. Where is your home, Boomer? If you don't mind my asking."

I said I was real tired, and pretended to doze off. I must have fallen asleep because when I opened my eyes again it was evening. The cabin door was still open and I could see that the sun had set. I thought about getting up, but when I raised up on my elbows the cabin started to sway again like a boat on water. I lay back down and stared out the door at the limb of a big old cottonwood tree that I could see outside.

While asleep I'd dreamed of Pepper over and over again. I kept trying to saddle her, but every time I reached for the cinch she shook herself and the saddle slid off. Then she would turn her head and laugh at me. Only it was my father's laugh that came from her bloody mouth.

When Ella came in carrying an armful of wood, she saw I was awake. "Hungry?" she asked.

"No," I said, "not very."

"Oh, you will be," Ella said.

After taking that Indian tea down I thought I'd lost my appetite for good.

I watched her stoke up the fire in the wood stove and fry a couple of steaks. And as the smell of cooked meat reached me, I thought I would go wild with hunger. When Ella broke eggs into the blackened frying pan, I knew I should be at the table to meet the food when it got there. I was halfway across the cabin before I realized I was naked.

Ella half-turned and gave me a slow up and down look, and said, "My, my."

I made it back to the bunk in three steps, hot with embarrassment. "Where's my clothes?"

"You don't have to shout," Ella said. "I buried your clothes out in the trash hole where they belong. They weren't even good for rags." She slid the pan off the heat and came back to a cowhide trunk near the bed. "I have some in here. They'll be a little roomy on you, but a sight better than what you had. I saved some of your socks and your lace-up shoes. Why don't you buy yourself a good pair of boots?"

I was too mad to answer. I didn't buy new clothes because I was down to my last two double eagles. I could hardly afford to buy canned food any more.

"I won't watch while you dress," Ella said, smiling. She set a pile of folded clothes on the bunk. "If you don't want cold food, you'll hurry."

I hurried. I had to roll the cuffs of the denim trousers up a little ways. The waist was half again too big for me. The shirt I put on was a light-colored cotton one, like cowboys wore. The sleeves were the right size, but the shoulders were too big. I was purely desperate for a belt but Ella hadn't put one out for me. I tucked the shirt in and held the trousers up, wondering whose clothes these were — her husband's probably.

It didn't take me long to go through the steak and half a dozen eggs. Ella had made cornbread and put several squares on my plate and a bowl of honey in front of me. I felt her watching me. Every time I glanced at her, she was smiling. To make conversation I asked where her husband was.

"I don't have a husband, Boomer. I'm not married."

31

That stopped me for a minute. "What are you doing out here in the desert?"

Her face broke into a smile and she laughed.

I felt myself blushing. "I mean, who owns this . . . this house? Your father?"

She shook her head. "No, Boomer, I'm alone here. This place is mine."

I stopped eating. I had never heard of such a thing. Women couldn't own property. Everybody knew that. I told her so.

"Maybe it's that way where you come from," she said, "but out here women can own property. We can vote, too."

Vote? I had never even thought of such a thing before. The whole idea was wilder than a burned lizard. But then I decided there probably wasn't much to vote on in a place like Wyoming, anyway. I sure hadn't seen anything worth voting for. And as for owning land, who cared if a woman owned a piece of the desert?

"You see, Boomer, I've claimed a quarter section here. If I can prove it up, I'll get to keep the whole hundred and sixty acres. It's good land."

"Good land!" I blurted. The farther west I'd ridden, the worse the land had become. The last good piece I'd seen was that basin where the white-painted ranch was.

Ella smiled at me as though she knew something I didn't know. "It's a little different down here than where you were when White Wolf found you." She had opened a can of peaches. She dished some into a bowl and handed it to me. "When you're through eating, come on outside and I'll show you."

"Who's White Wolf?"

"Don't you remember being found by an Indian?" She looked at me pitifully. "White Wolf found you yesterday. He saved your life."

I remembered, but my mind had been holding it back where it wouldn't bother me. It was bothering me now.

"That Indian killed my mare," I said.

"Boomer," Ella said softly, "he had to. He told me your mare was dying."

"I didn't think so," I said.

Ella reached over and held my hand. "I'll tell you one thing. White Wolf would never kill a horse unless he had to. He loves horses. He'd steal a horse before he'd kill one."

I knew she was watching me, but I didn't look up at her. "I don't know," was all I could say. But I did know. I'd done the worst thing that Boomer's father said a man could do. I'd mistreated a horse. My mare was dead because of what I'd done.

Ella must have guessed that I'd lost my appetite. "Come on outside before it gets dark," she said.

I must have stood up too fast because a dizzy spell hit me and about knocked me over. When I grabbed for the edge of the rough pine table to steady myself, I lost my trousers. I reached down and pulled them back up, feeling more embarrassed than dizzy now.

"Are you all right?" Laughter was not far out of her voice.

I said, "I sure could use a belt."

"Well, I reckon so," she said. Then she did laugh. "You sure could." She took a coil of cotton rope hanging from a nail on the log wall. I'd seen plenty of that white rope before. My father had it in his store. Ella cut a length and gave it to me. "Try that. It won't look like much, but it'll do the job. You sure you're feeling all right?"

"Yes, ma'am," I said as I guided the cotton rope through my belt loops and tied it in front. I was afraid if I told her anything else, she would pour some more Indian tea down me. I didn't want to lose all that steak and eggs.

When I stepped out the door of the cabin I saw a sight that almost put me in a daze again. For instead of seeing the desert, I saw a rich, grassy valley. I breathed in and smelled the moist evening air. The one cottonwood tree I'd seen from where I lay on the bunk inside the cabin was part of a long grove of trees that followed a river down the length of the valley. I saw this as I followed Ella across the yard to a field of high grass that almost hid a pair of wagon ruts. The ruts ran up and down the valley as far as I could see.

The mat of tall grass stretched nearly all the way from the tree line to the steep red cliffs that marked the far side of the valley. At the base of those cliffs clumps of sagebrush sprung up, a reminder of what the country becomes without water. Looking back at the cottonwoods I saw the shining river in breaks in the trees — the Sweetwater River, Ella called it.

Set away from the low cabin was a big barn with a pole corral butting up against it. Inside the corral I saw two horses. From the look of the raw lumber of the barn I could tell it was much newer than the cabin.

Ella pointed down the valley. "You can see some of my cattle down there. See those dark humps? They're bedding down now. And do you see that outgrowth of red rock down there? That's near the south boundary of my claim. The north boundary is just past the cabin here. When I prove up, I'll own this land from the cliffs over there to the west all the way to this bank of the Sweetwater."

She paused, then asked, "How do you like the place?"

It was the most beautiful valley I'd ever seen, the kind you might dream about after reading a book. "I like it fine," I said.

"You asked why I'm here, Boomer. I reckon it does seem strange to you, seeing as how you don't know me. One reason is that I'm trying to make a new life for myself. But the reason behind that one goes back to something my daddy always said. He said you can divide the people of the world up into those who own land and those who don't. And those who own land will never have to depend on anybody else. To my daddy, owning land meant freedom. That was his philosophy. I reckon it has stuck with me. I don't want to have to depend on other folks any more. I just want something I can call my own, some piece of land that will be mine as long as I live. Does that make any sense to you, Boomer?"

"Yes," I said.

We walked back to the cabin in the gathering darkness. Ella brought a lantern and an armful of blankets from inside the cabin and I followed her to the barn. By the swaying light of the lantern I saw the two horses standing close together inside the corral. On the other side of the barn a small chicken coop loomed in the near darkness. In the barn Ella held the lantern over a rawhide bunk that had been built against the wall of the first stall. I knew then the barn was new. It smelled more like lumber than manure.

"You'll have privacy out here, Boomer," Ella said, handing me the lantern. She spread the blankets over the bunk. "I don't know how much water the roof will shed, but it isn't likely to rain tonight." She glanced up into the shadows cast by the lantern light. "This time of year you never know, though. If it does rain and if you start getting wet, you scoot right into the cabin, hear? You're still in a weakened state. I won't have you taking cold."

I was surprised that she would leave her door unlocked.

"Folks don't lock doors in these parts," Ella laughed. "Boomer, you're from a city, aren't you?"

I wished I'd kept my mouth shut instead

37

of showing off my ignorance.

"You don't mind sleeping out here, do you, Boomer?"

"No," I said, trying to make my voice deep. "I've been on my own for a long time."

"You've come a long ways?"

I nodded, but when I looked at her I saw a strange look on her face, as though she was remembering something that was important to her. The yellow lantern light cast deep shadows in her face and made her eyes shine.

"Well, I reckon you won't be here for long," she said softly. "After you get another good meal or two in you, you'll be itching to move along and get to where you were going, won't you?"

When Ella left I undressed, blew out the lantern, and climbed into the bunk. After all those nights of sleeping on the ground, it was pure luxury to sleep on something that was flat from head to toe.

As I lay in the quiet darkness of the barn my thoughts were mixed and running together. I thought of losing Pepper and wished I could wake up and find her waiting for me as she always did when she was alive. Then my mind skipped to the valley as I'd seen it this evening and the idea that a woman was alone here, making a claim on a piece of land and owning cattle like a man. That was wilder than a burned lizard for sure.

I hadn't lain there long when I heard a rider come into the yard. I sat up and looked out through a crack between the boards. I didn't see anything until the door of the cabin opened. Yellow light spilled out, showing up a cowboy. He was tying his horse to the tie post in front of the low cabin.

"Why, howdy, Buck," Ella said. She stood in the doorway, wearing a long nightgown. Her hair was combed out and fluffed around her face and shoulders. "You working out of the south camp this month?"

The cowboy mumbled something as he walked back to his horse and opened a saddlebag. When he stepped through the patch of light to the cabin door, I saw he was carrying a long-necked amber bottle.

I remember climbing back under the blankets, thinking I would stay awake until the cowboy rode off. But I didn't make it. I heard a rooster crowing and my eyes blinked against daylight.

CHAPTER III

I had a purely wild thirst that morning. My lips were cracked open and bleeding again. During breakfast I tasted blood with every bite I took. Ella had made enough breakfast for three men — eggs, ham, hot bread with honey, and a big, blackened pot of coffee. It was the kind of coffee that gets added to every morning, but the grounds never get thrown out.

Ella didn't say anything about the man who came to visit her last night, and I didn't ask, though I was curious. I was surprised to find myself wishing she didn't have any men friends.

After breakfast Ella brought a jar of cream from the medicine shelf. She spread the stuff on my lips, telling me to try not to swallow it or it would make me sick. I didn't say so, but I thought the cream couldn't be any worse than Indian tea. She wanted to know all about how I felt, asking me questions about my aches and pains like a doctor would. I guessed she was comparing my answers to the symptoms described on the labels of patent medicine bottles.

I told her I was feeling as good as new. I didn't want her to worry over me for fear she would prescribe another dose of Indian tea. To head her off from such an idea, I asked if I could do some chores as payment for the trouble and extra work I caused her.

"No, Boomer," she said, "I don't want you to even think about doing any work today. You're too weak now. Yesterday you were damn near dead. I'll never forget how poorly you looked the first time I laid eyes on you. I didn't know whether I should put you to bed or start digging your grave."

"I'm feeling all right now," I said. "I ought to be doing something. You must have plenty of chores that need doing around here."

"Oh, hell, Boomer," Ella said, throwing up her hands. "I got more things to do around this place than I'll ever get done."

Ella's language surprised me at first. I'd never heard a woman swear before. But hearing those words come from Ella didn't seem so bad somehow. I could tell it was her natural way of talking. You couldn't hold that against anyone, not even a woman.

"One thing you can do, Boomer, is to draw up some water so we can clean these dishes. I hate seeing dirty dishes around the place. Makes me think somebody's sick." She put her hand under my chin and studied my face. "Is that cream working?"

I said it was, but my lips were still sore. At least I wasn't tasting blood any more. I still felt dried out and thirsty, but now I was too full to drink anything.

After the dishes were cleaned I moped around until midmorning. I began to feel restless and itchy to be doing something. I went to the woodpile at the side of the cabin and split some logs. Ella came out to see what I was doing and I thought she was going to tell me to stop, but she just looked at me as I worked, shaking her head. Then she went back inside.

About an hour later I heard a rider coming down the road. He turned in at the yard. I stepped out far enough from the side of the cabin to get a look at him, sort of expecting to see the same cowboy who had been here last night.

Only this man was no cowboy. He wore denim trousers, a plain cotton shirt, and boots, all right, but he was hatless and had a wild look about him, like he had just ridden out of a storm. His eyes bulged out of his head as though he could see through a thing. I think it was his eyes and a bushy head of hair that made him look so wild. He looked like he hadn't had a trim for a year.

Ella must have heard him ride in for she stepped out of the cabin, drying her hands on a towel.

"Goddammit, Ella!" the man shouted. "We got a thing or two to talk over. I mean to tell you —"

"Goddam you yourself, Chase Malone," Ella shouted back. "You got no call to come into my yard yelling at me. I ain't done a thing to you."

"I know it," Chase Malone shouted, "that's the whole goddam problem. You and Buck are getting along like a pair of songbirds, and that leaves me out of the picture. Me!"

"You don't own me, Chase Malone," Ella said. "You never have, you never will."

"But Buck Stone will, won't he?" Chase Malone said. He wasn't shouting as loud any more, but he was still in a rage. His eyes looked like a couple of pale eggs ready to fall out of his face.

"Who told you that?" Ella asked, laughing. "Did Buck say that?"

"No!" Chase Malone roared. Then he

added in a lower voice, "Well, what if he did? He ought to know, hadn't he?"

"Buck doesn't know any more than you do, Chase," Ella said. "A man as smart as you ought to have that figured out by now."

That got Chase Malone to shouting again. He was on one of the biggest saddle horses I'd ever seen, and that horse danced under him like his hoofs were on fire. "Ella, you're the damnedest woman that ever lived. You told me I was your man, now you go mixing it up with another man. I ought to —"

Ella took a threatening step toward Chase Malone, and she was shouting now and pointing at him. "I never told you you was my man. You ain't good enough. By God, you men sure can dream things up, can't you?"

"I remember you telling me that I was the best man you'd ever —"

Ella broke in, "So you let it go to your head, did you?"

"You meant it, though, when you said it."

"How do you know?" Ella said. "Anybody can make a mistake."

Chase Malone swore at that. His horse danced sideways, toward me. The rider didn't see me, but the horse did. He shied back in surprise and pawed the air like I was the devil with his name on my list. Chase Malone reined the horse down and glanced away from Ella long enough to see what was bothering the animal.

"Who the hell is that?" he shouted.

Ella didn't even look back at me. "Jesse James," she said.

"Who is that kid? What the hell is going on around here?"

"Nothing you need to worry about," Ella said. "Is that why you rode down here? To tell everybody about my love life and to see who's visiting me?"

Chase Malone was breathing hard while he tried to talk. He was having trouble holding his big horse still. He started to speak a couple of times before he finally got it out:

"Reese Clarke's got a bee in his ass. He'll probably be stopping by here today or tomorrow. I thought you ought to know that."

"I already know it," Ella said defiantly. "Buck Stone told me last night."

Chase Malone swore and pulled his jittery horse around hard and rode out of the yard, churning dust and sending chickens squawking and scurrying.

"Come back when you can stay longer," Ella called after him.

When she turned and walked back toward the cabin, I was surprised to see a smile on her face. I had thought she was mad enough at that man to shoot him.

"That was my neighbor, Chase Malone," she said to me. "When he's in one of his shouting moods, you have to shout back at him. Otherwise he won't respect you."

The man named Reese Clarke came that afternoon. I had carried several buckets of water up from the pump and filled Ella's washtub. She was scrubbing clothes on the washboard when a black two-wheeled buggy pulled by a matched pair of sleek black horses turned into the yard.

Ella straightened up and dried the palms of her hands on her cotton dress. The man who stepped out of the buggy was a small man with a tight smile. He wasn't any taller than I was, which made him shorter than Ella by a couple of inches. He wore a dark broadcloth suit and vest, black gloves and boots, and a high black Stetson. For some reason the outfit made him look smaller than he was, and as he walked toward us with quick little steps and a stiff smile on his face that might have been painted on, he reminded me of a midget or a circus freak.

"Good afternoon," he said through his teeth. His pale-eyed glance passed us as he looked down toward the barn.

"Good afternoon, Mr. Clarke," Ella said. Her voice sounded hollow and she stood too still. It wasn't until then that I realized how tense she was.

"Fine day, today," Reese Clarke said. He spoke in a small, raspy voice. "That's quite a barn there, new as can be."

Ella kept her gaze on the man instead of the barn.

"That's quite a barn," he said again. "Who built it?"

"Chase Malone," Ella said.

"Yessir, that's a fine, big barn," Reese Clarke said. "What do you aim to do with it?"

The question was so silly that at first I thought he was joking. The smile was still frozen on his face as he looked back at us. Then I saw Ella's strained face and I knew the question was meant to be hostile and somehow threatening.

Reese Clarke didn't wait for an answer. "You must think you've added a fair amount of value to this little piece of land with that big barn. I suppose you expect me to up my price."

"My quarter section ain't for sale, Mr. Clarke," Ella said. "You know that."

"Then why build such a barn?"

"Because of the Homestead Law," she said. "I have to put up a building of some kind to prove up."

"Prove up," Reese Clarke said. "You won't last another winter."

Ella didn't answer.

Reese Clarke started to say something else to her, but then he looked at me and his smile widened. "How do you figure into this, boy?"

I didn't know what he meant by *this*. I looked back into his pale eyes, but I couldn't match his stare. It was like trying to stare down a carp. When I didn't answer, Ella spoke up:

"He's the hired hand."

"Is he now," Reese Clarke said. "How old are you, boy?"

"Seventeen," I lied.

"You're scrawny for that age," he said. "But my son was always scrawny, too. He would have been fourteen this year." He paused as though he expected me to ask him something. Then he went on: "I lost my boy, lost both my beloved wife and son from sickness — Injun sickness. Injuns are carriers of deadly sicknesses and my wife and son fell victim to them."

I didn't understand why he was telling me about his family. But maybe he didn't, either. For it seemed to me that he caught himself, and his cold eyes shot back at Ella.

"What are you doing out here," he said, "a woman like you?"

"What do you mean, a woman like me?"

"You know what I mean," Reese Clarke said. "I never heard of a decent woman taking up her own homestead — legal or otherwise."

"I'm here legal," Ella said. "So is Chase Malone. We registered our claims with the land office in Sunbonnet."

Reese Clarke smiled again. "I'll grant you that you may get by with these shenanigans under a territorial government. But when statehood comes, Lord help you. You'll find out who's in the driver's seat in a hurry. Squatters like you won't last an hour."

"We ain't squatters, Mr. Clarke," Ella said.

He nodded. "No, you're more than that. You're a pair of lawbreakers who were run out of Sunbonnet."

"That ain't true. You know that ain't true."

Reese Clarke said, "You and Malone run cattle in this valley with fuzzy brands or no brands at all. And you're a temptress who leads my riders astray. Malone sells his liquor and you sell your flesh to gain —"

Ella's hand flew out and slashed back across Reese Clarke's face in a blow almost as loud as a shot. Staggered, Reese Clarke fell back a step and his feet tangled before he caught his balance. A cloud of dust floated up over his polished black boots and dulled their shine. I glanced at Ella and saw a look of disbelief and surprise on her face. But when I looked back at Reese Clarke his pale eyes were fixed on Ella and tears came from the eye on the side of his face that had suddenly become red as blood. His small hand came up and brushed the gleaming moisture away.

I heard Reese Clarke's raspy voice say, "You'll not stay here." Then he turned and strode to his buggy. It squeaked when he climbed in. I watched the buggy make a tight circle in the yard, then a whip popped against a rump and the little buggy nearly flew from the yard.

"Oh . . ." Ella said. "Oh . . ."

"You hit him," I said.

She nodded slowly. "Oh, how that man scares me."

"You didn't act scared," I said. I followed her into the cabin where she sank into a chair near the rough pine table. Her face was drawn and I thought she looked faint.

"Who was that man?" I asked.

"Reese Clarke," she said weakly. "He owns the C Bar Ranch west of here."

"Why doesn't he want you to stay in this valley?"

Ella shook her head. "I reckon he thinks he owns it. It's a long story, Boomer."

I could tell she wasn't in a mood to talk about it, but I wanted to say something that would make her feel better.

"I wasn't scared," I said. "I was more scared of Chase Malone than I was of Mr. Clarke."

Ella smiled at me and then laughed softly. She got up and poured herself a cup of coffee, adding a shot of whiskey. "I reckon I can see why you would be, Boomer," she said as she sat down again. "But if you knew Chase Malone better, you'd like him. He's a man who keeps his cards face up. If he's mad, he shows it. If he's happy, he shows it. But with a joker like Reese Clarke you can't tell what the bastard's thinking. When he's mad, he smiles. I don't know what he does when he's happy."

Ella perked up as she got to talking. After she finished her coffee we left the cabin and walked through the cottonwood grove to the bank of the Sweetwater River. It was cool there in the late afternoon shade and the air smelled moist and sweet. The river ran flat and shiny smooth, making only low sounds where it bubbled around boulders. We sat on the bank and watched the water for a time. Ella sat with her knees under her chin and after a while she talked about how quiet it was beside the river and how the flowing water had a way of making you feel peaceful and calm.

I sat there as long as I could without throwing stones into the water. But when I couldn't stand it any longer, I picked up a round one and pitched it. When it splashed, I knew the water was deeper than it looked. I threw another one. Then Ella began talking to me about herself.

"I've just been thinking about how unhappy I was at your age, Boomer. I don't remember ever being happy as a girl. Oh, there was probably times when I was. But they haven't stuck in my memory. I believed I wouldn't be happy until I got grown. I thought of growing up as waiting to be happy. I remember daydreaming that when I was grown a handsome man would come along like something magical and take me away and I would be happy from then on.

"But there ain't much magic in this world. You got to work and fight for what you want. I was raised in a big family — three boys and five girls. We had a farm back in Iowa. All of us worked, boys and girls alike, sunup to sundown. It seems like that was all we ever did: work and sleep, work and sleep, church on Sundays.

"Well, when I was sixteen Daddy died of consumption. My oldest brother, Willard, took over the farm. Willard had a mean streak in him and he had a mean way of bossing us kids. I never liked being bossed at all. Daddy had a way of telling us what to do without bossing us. But after he died Mother always sided with Willard, knowing all the time how mean he was. I reckoned she figured she had to side with him to keep the farm together. Willard got worse and worse until finally I couldn't take it no longer. So you know what I did, Boomer?"

I watched a rock I'd thrown sail high up over the water and splash in a pool behind a boulder. I wondered if you could ever hit a fish doing that. I shook my head at Ella's question.

"I reckon you could make a pretty fair guess, Boomer."

Part of my thoughts had drifted away with the river. I had to think back to figure out what she was asking. But then she answered the question herself:

"I ran off from home."

By the way she was looking at me I knew she had me figured out. She'd read me like a map. And I guessed that she had another purpose in talking to me besides telling me her life story.

"One Sunday afternoon I packed my things in a hatbox and walked down the road to the junction. I'd told everybody I was going to visit a girl friend, as I often did on Sundays. I remember stopping once or twice and looking back at the house. The place needed paint, but Willard wouldn't spend the money for it. All he could do was complain about the price of seed. So every year the house got more run down."

Ella stared out across the river for a long moment as though she was looking back at that farmhouse in Iowa. "Anyhow, Boomer, I've never been back since, never

54

even wanted to. I was happy to get out. It was like getting out of jail. I'll bet you know that feeling, Boomer."

I knew the feeling, all right, but hearing the easy way she talked about it made me feel funny. It was like she had forgotten something important, something she had fought for. I had hard feelings toward my father and I believed I always would.

Ella laughed absently at something she had thought of. "I never even sent a letter home until I turned eighteen. I wrote from Denver, but I didn't put down a return address. I didn't want Willard coming after me. Besides, I was working in a place my mother wouldn't have approved of, if you know what I mean."

I felt Ella's eyes on me as I looked out across the water. I wasn't exactly sure what she did mean, but I wasn't going to show my ignorance by guessing out loud.

"I felt grown up when I sent that letter," Ella went on, "but now after all these years I know that I got grown when I packed up that hatbox and walked away from the house. I was full grown then whether I knew it or not."

When she quit talking I was afraid she would start asking me questions about where I was from and what I was doing out in the middle of Wyoming Territory and so on. But I was wrong. She fell silent. After a while she stood up, stretched, and said it was time to start supper. It wasn't until then that I realized she had given me the chance to tell her about myself. But I hadn't done it, and she wasn't going to pry.

I followed her up the path that led through the trees to the cabin. But before we came out of the grove, a blur of flesh and buckskin leaped out from the shadows, crossed the path, and disappeared. I must have cried out for Ella turned back and took my arm.

"It's all right," she said.

I couldn't catch my breath to speak. We walked ahead together and when we came out of the trees, I looked down past the barn and saw White Wolf. Ella saw him, too. He stood in the shadows between two big cottonwood trees, as still as the trees themselves. When Ella called to him, he turned and stepped back into the grove. I lost sight of him.

Struggling to catch my breath, I said, "There was another one, too."

"I know," Ella said, "I heard him running in the brush."

"What were they doing here?"

Ella shrugged. She wasn't frightened at all. "White Wolf has a camp a little ways downriver that he uses once or twice a year. He probably walked up here just to see what was going on."

But that night, long after I'd gone to bed, I lay awake in the quiet darkness of the barn, remembering with fear how the Indian had come out of the trees and run past me faster than I'd ever seen a human move.

Before I drifted off to sleep thoughts of home and of my father got mixed in with my remembering the story Ella had told of her girlhood. She said she had become grown the day she ran off from home. For a moment I tried to think the same had happened to me. But I knew it hadn't. I felt the same as I ever had — not like a man. For I knew that becoming a man would be something I could feel, like when my voice changed or when hair started growing on my legs. No, I was still a boy going on sixteen, waiting to become a man.

CHAPTER IV

White Wolf came back in the morning. Ella and I had done the chores — cleaned up the breakfast dishes, fed the chickens, and tended the horses. The two geldings were named Billy and Bobby. They were a pair of old team animals that Ella used with her buckboard.

By midmorning Ella was in the yard scrubbing out clothes on a washboard and I was at the woodpile beside the cabin, working up some stove wood. Then, with the ax poised high over my head, something caught my eye, something that hadn't been there before. I glanced up just as I started to swing the ax and saw White Wolf standing between the same two cottonwood trees that he had stood between last evening. My aim was spoiled and the ax came down at an angle and slid off the side of the log I was splitting.

"Ella," I said, as White Wolf came into the yard.

She looked up and saw him. White Wolf walked toward her, his moccasined feet spread wide, wearing his stained buckskin shirt and sun-bleached army trousers. And even as Ella greeted him and he grinned at her, I could not look at White Wolf without seeing a savage, without feeling a wild sense of fear and a sudden weakness in my legs.

"The boy lives," White Wolf said, looking at me.

Ella straightened up from the washboard and looked at me, too. "He's alive and kicking. But he wouldn't be if you hadn't found him when you did."

White Wolf stood in the yard and watched Ella wring out the last of the clothes and hang them on the clothesline. When she finished she went inside the cabin and was gone several minutes. I had gone back to cutting wood, but I felt White Wolf watching me.

When Ella came outside she brought a wicker basket full of big sugar cookies, three cups of coffee, and a bowl of sugar. She and White Wolf sat on the grass in the shade of the cabin.

"Come and sit," Ella said to me.

I sat beside Ella, keeping the wicker basket between White Wolf and me. White Wolf grinned as he filled his cup of coffee half full of sugar. The coffee spilled over as

59

he raised it to his lips. He drank, slurping loudly. Ella winked when I looked at her in surprise.

"More coffee," White Wolf said when he had drained the cup. He held it out to Ella with one hand and took a handful of cookies with the other.

When Ella brought him another cup of coffee, White Wolf loaded it up the same way. Ella asked him some questions, but he hardly answered at all. White Wolf wasn't interested in talking and eating at the same time, I guessed. After Ella asked him where he was camped, he jerked his head down-stream. She asked if he had his wives with him. White Wolf nodded as he punched two more cookies into his mouth.

"Why didn't you bring them up here?" she asked "Your family is always wel-come."

White Wolf shrugged and spoke around the cookies: "Squaws thieving bitches."

That made Ella laugh as hard as I'd ever seen her laugh. White Wolf got to laugh-ing, too, but lost some of the cookies when his mouth opened. He clapped his hand to his mouth like a child might. I was amazed. White Wolf was a terrible savage one minute, and a child the next.

After White Wolf had eaten and drunk

his fill he belched, took a pipe from a pocket in his army trousers, and fired it. He smoked a white man's pipe, a blond one that curved down and back up into a huge bowl. It looked too big for a man to hold in his teeth. But White Wolf didn't have any trouble with it. Smoke poured out of his mouth like out of a steam engine.

Ella said to me, "I gave him that pipe, Boomer. I bought it in town last fall. It was made in Scotland. He sure is proud of it."

From the expression on Ella's face as she watched White Wolf smoke, I thought she was as proud of the pipe as White Wolf was.

After smoking and digesting for quite a while, White Wolf began to talk. He carried on for a long time. Whenever I didn't understand what he was saying, I'd look at Ella and she would explain in a quick whisper what she thought he meant. I got most of it on my own, though. I understood his words better than the first time I'd heard him speak. I wondered where he had learned so much English, but I knew this wasn't the right time to ask.

As a boy White Wolf had no name. Among the Cheyennes a name was something a man earned. It was like a title.

When White Wolf was judged ready to enter manhood, he had a council with the medicine man of his tribe. The medicine man gave him a pouch filled with secret things. This stuff was the great medicine that would guide him safely through a long life in which he would meet many enemies and dangers from evil spirits.

White Wolf still carried the pouch. He lifted up his buckskin shirt and showed it to me. It was nothing but a small leather bag, hung from his neck by a thong.

White Wolf, as a boy with no name, went deep into the forest where he could be alone with the spirits that lived there. He had been told the spirits would come to him. They would tell him what kind of life he would lead as a man of the tribe and as a warrior. White Wolf fasted for three days, taking only water. No spirits came to him. He was saddened and ashamed. The boy began to fear the spirits were staying away because they saw death's shadow on him.

But on the fourth day one of the greatest of all spirits came to the place in the forest where he sat waiting. The spirit was in the form of a white wolf. This spirit circled him three times. The boy was frightened of the wolf, yet he made himself still. The wolf's coat was as white as snow in the sunlight; his eyes shone red and hot as two coals in a night fire. Soon the boy fell under the spell of this spirit's great beauty.

The white wolf said to the boy, "You have waited for me with the patience of a man. I have watched you. Now I have come to tell you I am your spirit. I am your spirit alone. We are one.

"You will take my name. You will be known by all the people as White Wolf. You will have a long life as a great warrior. One day you will be chosen to lead the people. You will be White Wolf, the leader. And you will be the greatest leader of all time. You will take the people on their longest and hardest journey. Many will die. There will be great sadness and death. Yet you must lead them on. The people will follow you because you have my strength.

"One day you will find strange humans who have done an evil thing. They have the hide of a white wolf. All the men of this tribe must be killed as they killed the spirit of the white wolf. You must do this. You will know the time in which to do it.

"You will have much trouble in your long life. But one day you will find a strange boy who has no people. You will know this boy because he will fear you as you fear me. You will save him from death three times. After you do this your life will no longer be troubled. Follow my spirit, young White Wolf, for I am the leader of leaders."

White Wolf said all the spirit's predictions had come true in his lifetime. He was a great warrior. And he became the leader of his people. When they were driven to the Indian Territories, it was White Wolf who led his people back to their homelands. This was the long and sad journey the spirit had spoken of. And during this journey a family of whites was found to have the hide of a freshly killed white wolf. There were three males in the family. One was a small boy. White Wolf wanted only the men killed, for surely it was one of them who had killed the spirit of the wolf. But the attack went so well that a few of the younger warriors did not stop until all the whites were dead, a family of nine.

After returning to the homeland White Wolf's troubles began. One day he and the warriors drank from the white man's bottle and a fight was started. A young warrior named Starved Bear believed White Wolf was no longer powerful. He recalled that on the journey from the south they had seen the hide of a slain white wolf. This could only mean the spirit inside White

Wolf was dead, too. White Wolf denied this. He accused Starved Bear of being nothing but a killer of women. In the fight that followed White Wolf killed Starved Bear and condemned his spirit to live in the ashes of dead fires of his enemies.

For the crime of murder White Wolf was banished from his tribe. As the spirit in the forest had told him, White Wolf was having great trouble in his long life. But then he had found a strange boy with no people. He had saved this boy from death.

White Wolf looked at me and said, "I am White Wolf who saves the boy."

It wasn't until then that I understood White Wolf was talking about me. I was the boy with no people. White Wolf looked at me solemnly as though it was my turn to say something. I looked at Ella, but she shrugged.

Finally I said, "Thank you, White Wolf," and I realized that was the first time I had spoken to the man who had saved my life. I said it again, louder, "Thank you, White Wolf."

White Wolf nodded once, stood up, and walked back into the cottonwood grove. He paused between the same two trees where I'd seen him standing last evening and then again today as I was cutting wood. He disappeared into the shadows and for a moment I thought he was gone. But then he came back, leading a saddled, whiteheaded roan pony.

"I kill horse of the boy. I give him another."

About the same time that it occurred to me it was strange for an Indian pony to be saddled, I saw that it was my own saddle on him. My bridle was tied to the horn.

I heard Ella swear softly before she said, "Now, White Wolf, you needn't worry over the boy. He'll get himself another horse, won't you, Boomer?" She motioned for me to speak up.

I nodded, but I couldn't take my eyes off the roan pony.

Ella said, "The boy knows you only killed his mare because you had to. Don't you, Boomer?"

I nodded again. I couldn't figure out why Ella was so intent on keeping White Wolf from giving me the pony. I was sure ready to take him. He was a beautiful, small-hoofed and graceful-looking pony. He wasn't jittery exactly, but he wasn't tame by a long shot, either. Every little sound made his ears perk and his eyes would roll a little. Both his ears were notched in a strange way. A deep V was cut from the top of each one. And I had never seen a horse with his coloring. He was pure roan except for his head. In a line in front of his ears to the back of his jaw he was white, as white as if he'd dunked his whole head into a bucket of whitewash.

I remembered reading in a library book that horses meant wealth to an Indian. Maybe Ella was trying to keep White Wolf from giving away more than he could afford.

Then I heard Ella say softly, "I reckon you're going to have to take that damned horse, Boomer."

I tore my eyes away from the pony and looked at White Wolf. A purely angry look was on his face. He held out the pony's lead rope for me to take, but he was staring off at the red cliffs of the Sweetwater Valley as though his worst enemy was sitting out there calling him names.

But when I took the rope from his hand, his expression suddenly changed and he was happy again. White Wolf nodded and smiled at us as though we were good friends that he had not seen for a long time. Then he gestured goodbye and walked back into the cottonwood grove.

The pony craned his head around and watched White Wolf disappear in the shadows of the trees. When he figured out he was going to be left alone, he struggled against the rope, trying to follow White Wolf.

I pulled his head back around and reached out to stroke his nose, but the pony jerked away in fear, his eyes rolling back like eggs. I pulled on the rope hard, but for a moment I didn't think I could hold him. He was strong for a pony.

Ella said quickly, "Walk him around. Let him move some."

I led him in a big circle around the yard. He calmed a little but his skin jumped nervously. On the fourth time around his head was still bobbing, but I could tell that he wasn't as nervous. After another couple of turns around the yard, he began to prance.

Ella laughed. "He's nothing but a show-off."

"Isn't he beautiful?" I said.

Ella's smile faded. "I reckon you know you shouldn't plan to keep him, don't you?"

That stopped me in my tracks. "Why?"

"He's probably stolen."

I hadn't seen a brand on him, but now I looked again. I didn't see any markings.

Ella said, "White Wolf probably stole that pony from another Indian. He's done it before. He trades them to the officers at Fort America. Chase Malone can tell you all about that."

"You mean White Wolf steals horses from his own people?" I asked. "Why?"

"I reckon he wants to remind the Cheyenne that they made a bad mistake by throwing him away from his tribe. He steals a prize horse now and then to keep them from forgetting."

I had begun walking the pony again when Ella said, "I can see from the look on your face that you want to keep him."

"I don't care if he's stolen."

She said, "But somebody else will."

"Who?"

"The Indian White Wolf stole him from," Ella said patiently. "That's a fine horse. Somebody's likely to come looking for him."

"I'm going to keep him," I said. "White Wolf gave him to me, and I'm going to keep him. I'll ride away tonight."

"Oh, no, you won't," Ella said. "I didn't nurse you back to health to have you ride back out there to get lost again. You must have a mighty short memory."

The meaning behind her words hurt me more than what she said. I didn't look at her. For I knew she believed I was nothing but a helpless boy who would get lost and mistreat his horse. I wanted to prove to her that she was wrong.

I led the pony up to her and stopped. "But what can I do?"

She started to say something, but she stopped. She looked at the pony, then at me. "Come on, let's take a walk."

We walked north, following the wagon ruts up the valley. The afternoon sun was almost hot, but it was a gentle, spring heat that felt good as it seeped in through my clothes and skin. The air smelled good with the fresh smell of growing grass. The pony followed along, keeping slack in the lead rope, as though he was interested in where we were going. I asked Ella, but she only said we were going to see a man about a horse.

Then up ahead against the line of cotton-wood trees I saw a building. It was false-fronted and the yellow lumber showed that it was new. Over the doorway a crooked sign read: *SALOON GEN. MERC. POST OFFICE*. The building stood alone against the cottonwoods that bordered the river. I was about to ask who lived there when Ella picked up a stone and threw it at the building.

It was a long throw for a woman. But she

had plenty of range and the stone struck the false-front a couple of feet above the sign with a hollow *thunk.*

From inside came a long yell: "Elllaaaa!"

The man who came out on the porch was Chase Malone. He put his hands on hips and watched us as we walked toward him. He looked the same as the first time I'd seen him. His hair was as wild as a tangle of barbed wire and his eyeballs bulged out of their sockets like two marbles about to be shot.

Ella said, "Chase, when are you going to get that sign straightened?"

Chase Malone's face broke into a sudden smile. "You come on inside and drink up and then take a look at that sign. It straightens up every time."

Ella said she didn't doubt it. "Chase, I want you to meet a friend of mine. This is Boomer Jones. Boomer, meet the famous Chase Malone."

We shook hands formally. He said he was proud to make my acquaintance, then he stepped back and looked me over.

"I believe I've seen you somewhere before, Boomer."

Ella laughed. "Sure, you have. You saw him down at my place. You didn't stay long, but you saw him."

"I remember," Chase Malone said, "but it seems like I've seen him somewhere before that. I can't place him."

At first I'd felt nervous because I knew I was blushing. But when he said he had seen me before, my old fears washed back over me like a big wave of cold water. What if my father had sent out circulars with my picture on them? Maybe Chase Malone had been in a town somewhere and had seen one. I was trying to think of something to say that would head him off when Ella laughed.

"No," she said, "you haven't seen him. But you have seen the clothes he's wearing. They were in that last batch you brought down to have mended."

A quick smile lit Chase Malone's face again. "Why, sure. No wonder you look familiar, Boomer. You look like me — thirty years ago." He walked behind us. "Well, what have we here? That's a fine-looking pony, a Cheyenne war pony. How'd you get hold of him?"

"That's what we came to talk to you about, Chase," Ella said.

I asked excitedly, "How do you know he's a war pony?"

"You see those notches in his ears?" Chase Malone asked. "Those were cut in there so his owner can find his horse right away, even when it's dark. Oftentimes at night is when a man needs his top horse the most."

Ella told him how I had come to get the pony. She didn't mention that she suspected White Wolf had stolen him, but Chase Malone said exactly that.

"Yessir," Chase Malone said, running his hand along the pony's side, "when old White Wolf steals a horse, he doesn't take just any old plug — he cuts the best of the remuda."

I watched Chase Malone examine the pony. Then he did an amazing thing. He waved his hand to the ground in a sudden motion, as though he was trying to spook him. But the pony went to his knees and laid down, never taking his eyes off Chase Malone. When he raised his hand, palm up, and made a clucking sound in his mouth, the pony got back to his feet.

I thought only circus horses could do stunts like that. "Did White Wolf train him to do those tricks?"

"Those tricks, as you call them," Chase Malone said, "can mean life or death to a Cheyenne warrior. If he's on the run, he and his pony can hide behind a clump of brush that you wouldn't think could hide a mouse. No, some Indian spent months working on this pony, probably since he was a colt. I don't believe White Wolf has had him that long."

Ella asked, "Do you reckon his owner will come hunting for him?"

Chase Malone nodded. "From the way you described White Wolf trying so hard to give this pony away, I'd guess that he believes the owner will be coming after him. Or maybe White Wolf has spotted him already."

Ella said, "I just remembered something, Chase. Last night as Boomer and I were walking back to the cabin from the river, some Indian jumped out of the brush and ran in front of Boomer. I didn't see him, but I heard him. You don't reckon he could be the owner of this pony?"

"You didn't get a look at him?" Chase Malone asked me.

I shook my head. "It happened too fast."

"From the way he hollered," Ella said, "I thought he'd been bit by a rattler."

"I doubt that was the brave who lost his prize pony," Chase Malone said. "If it had been, he'd probably have taken your head off. More likely it was that loco Birdy."

"Who's he?" I asked.

"Not he," Chase Malone said, "she. White Wolf has a crazy niece or daughter named Spirit of the Bird, or some such name. I call her Birdy. I've never been straight on how she's related to White Wolf, but she's never too far away from him."

"That would be right," Ella said, "because right after that happened, we saw White Wolf standing off in the trees." Ella reached over to the pony and scratched him behind the jaw. "Boomer's got his heart set on keeping him, Chase."

"Can't blame you," he said. "This is a fine pony. He looks smart enough to talk."

Ella asked Chase Malone the same question I'd asked her: "But what can he do?"

I said, "I'll have to fight for him."

Chase Malone laughed. "Boomer, you sure got spirit. Now, I don't mean to down-talk you, but the truth is you wouldn't stand a chance against a full-grown Cheyenne warrior. If he was your own age, I'd put even money on you. But not a grown one, Boomer, not the Indian who must have owned this pony. He'd slice you six ways from Sunday and beat your head in with a rock before you could blink. I know. I soldiered against them."

He told me to tie the pony to the hitchrack and step inside. It was dark and cool in the building. As my eyes adjusted to the light I didn't see anything of a store or post office. It was a saloon with a plank bar supported by two large kegs. There was a scattering of tables and chairs across the floor. I smelled sawdust. I looked down and saw I was walking in the stuff.

Ella and I followed Chase Malone to the back of the saloon. He opened a door and motioned us into his living quarters. Long shafts of dust-filled afternoon light slanted through the windows. I saw a bunk and wood stove at one end of the room, a small dining table in the center, and at the far end was a huge rolltop desk and swivel chair. The wall behind the desk was lined with thick, leatherbound books all the way to the ceiling.

We sat at the dining table while Chase Malone poured three cups of the blackest coffee I'd ever seen. It looked like paint, only thicker.

"There's only one safe thing for you to do, boy," he said as he sat in the chair across from me. "Get that horse out of this region as fast as you can. What I'd recommend is to take him down to Sunbonnet and load him on the train. Ship him to Nevada. Or California."

After a long pause, Ella asked, "How about that, Boomer?"

I didn't have near enough money to do that. But instead of telling the truth, I said, "I'm not headed for Nevada or California."

"Where are you headed?" Chase Malone asked.

I shrugged and studied the coffee in my cup.

After a long silence during which I felt both of them looking at me, Chase Malone said, "Son, from your accent I'd guess you're from the East. Somewhere in New England, likely. What did you do? Did you run away and come out here thinking you'd become a cowboy?"

I couldn't look up at him or at Ella. I felt like I was burning up and drowning in sweat.

"Listen, Boomer," Ella said gently, "you can talk to us. We're not going to report you to anyone, no matter what you've done."

"That's right," Chase Malone said. "I didn't mean to ask so many questions. If you're on the dodge, just keep it to yourself."

I looked up and said, "I wanted to get a job as a cowboy, but I haven't had any experience."

Ella said to Chase Malone, "Maybe Buck would hire him on at the C Bar."

Chase Malone said dryly, "Buck Stone would do just about anything you asked of him, Ella."

"Now, Chase, don't start that."

Chase Malone studied me for a while, then said, "You won't find a better foreman to work under than Buck Stone. He's a fair man — goodhearted, too. That's more than can be said for Reese Clarke, that land-grabbing bastard who owns the C Bar. What it comes down to is that you'd be working for Reese Clarke. I'd hate to see any young man start out his working life that way."

Ella said, "But he'd be working under Buck, wouldn't he?"

Chase Malone nodded. "All the C Bar hands answer to Buck. He's made that ranch into what it is today. Everybody except Reese Clarke knows that. Buck has built that C Bar crew up to the place where he's carrying only top hands on the payroll. Even the wrangler is a first-rate cowboy. That means about the only job open to a boy like Boomer would be cook's helper. But even that's a start."

I said, "I planned to start out by working on a small ranch to get some experience."

Chase Malone smiled. "The work is about the same on any cattle ranch in these parts, Boomer. But you're in the wrong part of the country to find a small ranch. You might think about going down to Colorado. There are some small mountain ranches down there that might hire you on — although this is the time of year when plenty of experienced cowboys will be looking for work, too."

"I can't leave right now," I said. "I have a debt to pay Ella. I'm going to do chores —"

"You ain't in debt to me, Boomer," Ella said.

"You saved my life."

"No, I didn't. White Wolf did that."

"You fed me and put clothes on me," I said. I guessed I should have been grateful for the Indian tea, too, but I couldn't make myself say it.

"You don't owe me a thing," Ella said, trying to look stern.

But I said again, "I have to work off the debt."

Chase Malone grinned crookedly. "Looks like this is one argument you're going to lose, Ella."

She smiled, nodding slowly.

Chase Malone said, "Boomer, here's

something for you to think on. You probably know that Ella and I are proving up
bordering quarter sections here on the
Sweetwater. We run about thirty head
between us. That isn't much stock, but we
both have more work and chores than we
can handle. There is plenty of work
around here to keep another man busy. It
wouldn't be all cowboying work and we
couldn't pay top wages, but it would be a
start for you. Would you be interested in
such a proposition?"

Ella had been watching me while Chase
Malone was talking. She said, "I'm getting
used to having you around the place."

I didn't need time to think over that job
offer. "I'd like that fine," I said.

We shook hands on it, the three of us.

CHAPTER V

Ella laughed and said to me, "I reckon I was telling the truth when I told Reese Clarke you were my hired hand."

"Clarke stopped by, did he?" Chase Malone asked. "What did he want?"

"Same old thing," Ella said. "First he told me I didn't have a legal right to be here, then he offered to buy me out."

"What did you tell him?"

" 'No,' " she said. "But he downgraded me and I reckon I lost my temper."

Over bad coffee in the back of Chase Malone's saloon Ella told him about Reese Clarke's visit the day before. I was too wound up in my thoughts to pay much attention to what was being said. I saw myself riding that whiteheaded Indian pony up and down the Sweetwater Valley, checking fences and the condition of the cattle like a real cowboy would. I shot rattlesnakes and stopped stampedes by myself.

A raspy voice shouted from outside the saloon: "Malone!"

"Speaking of the devil," Ella said.

I followed Ella and Chase Malone through the saloon to the porch. They stepped out to the front edge of the porch, but I stayed back in the shadow of the doorway.

Half a dozen mounted cowboys were lined up in front of the saloon. Reese Clarke sat in his little buggy before the cowboys. All the cowboys were different in size and posture as they sat their saddles, yet they somehow looked alike. They all squinted and grimaced against the afternoon sunlight even though their hats were pulled low over their eyes. Those hats were battered and sweat-stained, and some had rattlesnake hatbands. All the cowboys wore bleached-out trousers and faded cotton shirts and boots with run-down heels. Several of the men had heavy, drooping mustaches. As my eyes passed down the line of men, I recognized the cowboy on the far end. He was Buck Stone.

Reese Clarke didn't get out of his buggy. He leaned forward and said, "I came by to give you fair warning, Malone. This saloon and sporting house you run is off limits to all C Bar riders. You've enticed my men in here and taken their money for the last time. You've poured that cheap liquor of yours down their throats."

"Hold on, Clarke," Chase Malone said. "If you want to put this place off limits to the C Bar, then go ahead. But, by God, don't accuse me of cheating men or poisoning them. The cowboys who come in here gamble with each other, not with me or any outsider. You ask any of those men you brought with you. They'll tell you. These are men out of the south camp, aren't they?"

Reese Clarke said, "You won't be seeing much of them any more."

"What did you do, fire them?" Chase Malone asked.

Reese Clarke shook his head. "I'm moving them up to the north camp. If any of them try to come back here, they'll be fired. They know that."

Chase Malone said to the cowboys, "Those of you who aren't already saints had better start getting used to wearing a robe."

The men laughed at that. Buck Stone smiled and shook his head. Reese Clarke smiled, too, but it was a different kind of smile and I knew he wasn't enjoying the joke.

"Malone, I'm going to make you the same offer I made the woman. You can take my price for this quarter section you're squatting on, or you can wait until the sheriff runs your ass out of the territory."

"You must be souring with age, Reese," Chase Malone said. "There was a time when you could ride into a man's yard and act decent."

"I talk to all trespassers the same way, Malone. I'll ask you again —"

"My answer is the same one Ella gave you," Chase Malone said. "My little piece of property isn't for sale."

"Then you'll have to suffer the consequences," Reese Clarke said.

"That almost sounds like a threat."

"Take it any way you like."

Buck Stone stayed back with the cowboys as if he didn't know Ella or Chase Malone at all. The riders had begun to fidget. One lanky cowboy took off his hat and seriously scratched his head. His forehead, above the crease left by the Stetson, was pure white. The skin on the rest of his face was the color of tanned hide. Another cowboy made a smoke and fired it by dragging a match down the bottom side of his denim trouser leg. When the match flared, a piece of sulphur must have hit the horse next to him for the animal squealed and reared. The rider brought him down and backed him out of the line. My own pony, tied at the rack, fussed and moved sideways to watch what was going on behind him.

Reese Clarke said, "If you think I'm going to be kindly to trespassers who are trying to cut the heart out of this valley, then you're wrong."

"Our claims are legal and you know it," Chase Malone said. "And since you're sitting on my land, I'd say you're the one who's trespassing."

Reese Clarke smiled his hard smile again. "You can talk big, but that won't change anything. I've tried to be fair with you. What happens from here on is out of my hands."

"What do you mean by that?" Ella asked.

Reese Clarke said, "I wondered how much longer you could hold your tongue, woman. It's fortunate for you that I'm a gentleman."

"I asked you what you meant by 'what happens from here on,'" Ella said.

"Just what I said. You're here illegally. The laws of the land will be enforced. It's out of my hands from here on. Is that simple enough for you to understand?"

"There's no need to insult the woman," Chase Malone said.

"I believe that would be impossible," Reese Clarke said, turning the buggy.

The cowboys fell in behind Reese Clarke's buggy and left the yard. But most of them smiled and waved now that Reese Clarke's back was turned. Buck Stone shrugged and looked up at the sky. I stepped out onto the porch and watched them until they were out of sight.

Ella said, "That man . . ."

"We've heard his song before," Chase Malone said. "Last winter he called us outlaws. Now we're trespassers. Next month it will be something else."

"It sounded like he had some idea about moving us out," Ella said. Then she laughed. "You sure pinned him back when you told him he was trespassing. I wish I could think of things to say that quick. You could have lit kindling off him."

Chase Malone looked up the valley where the men had ridden. Then he turned and walked to the doorway. "Step right in, folks, step right in," he said like a circus barker, "have a drink in the wildest cat house in the whole Sweetwater Valley."

We sat at a round table near the center of the saloon. Overhead I saw lanterns hung from wires that ran all the way to the ceiling. Chase Malone brought a bottle from the shelf behind the plank bar. In his free hand he carried three tin cups. When he sat down, he poured two of the cups half full, then shoved the third over to me.

"Do you drink Irish whisky?" he asked.

I shook my head.

"You mean you don't drink, or you don't drink Irish whisky?"

"No," I said.

"What the hell kind of answer is that?"

"I've never had any Irish whisky before," I said.

"What have you had?" Chase Malone asked.

I shrugged. I'd never drunk anything stronger than wine at communion.

"That means you had some kind of whiskey out behind the shed and you were too scared to read the label. Here, have a shot of Ireland, the best in the house."

He poured some in my cup. I watched Chase Malone and Ella drink theirs, then I tried it. It smelled wild, but swallowing the stuff was worse. It was like trying to swallow a tree limb. I choked and tears ran from my eyes. When Ella laughed, her voice sounded far away.

Chase Malone said, "Good, isn't it?"

My stomach felt like someone had pointed a shotgun down my throat and pulled the trigger.

"I won't buy cheap Irish whisky," Chase Malone said solemnly. "That stuff is hard on a man. But this Murphy's is top grade, fine and smooth as rain water."

"Are you all right, Boomer?" Ella asked.

"Sure, he's all right," Chase Malone said. "Why, I remember my first shot of Ireland . . ." He looked off into a corner of the saloon as though he was looking at a memory. Then he said, "Of course, what I remember most is when my father caught me drinking Bourbon at the age of thirteen. Oh, did the senator lay the whip on my bare bottom!"

Ella asked, "He whipped you for sipping some old Bourbon?"

"No," Chase Malone said, "he whipped me for adding water to his bottle to make up for what I'd taken. My ruining the whole bottle was what he whipped me for."

"Your father was a senator?" I asked.

"He was," Chase Malone said. "Served three terms in Washington. He was more honest than most men who run for public office."

I wanted to know more about his father, but Chase Malone got to talking about the first time he'd ever drunk any Irish whisky. A woman had poured it for him. "Ah, it's an experience a man doesn't forget."

I wasn't going to forget mine.

Ella and Chase Malone each had another session with Ireland, but I'd had enough. I waved the bottle away when Chase Malone pointed it at me. Nobody said anything for a while, so I went ahead and asked why Reese Clarke was so intent on getting them out of the valley. It seemed like a big valley to me.

Ella slammed her hand on the table and I realized she was getting a little drunk. "That's right, Boomer. Our two quarter sections ain't even a drop in a rain barrel to a cowman like Reese Clarke. He's plain greedy."

I picked up something Ella had hinted at earlier. "It sounded like Mr. Clarke might have some legal way of making you move. He kept talking about a sheriff."

"Reese Clarke has some funny ideas about laws," Chase Malone said. "He figures laws are good as long as he agrees with them. But when a law comes up that he can't get along with, then he overlooks it and makes up his own law. In years past the C Bar has used this valley for winter range. A few other cowmen have, too, when they smelled a bad winter coming. It's protected down here and when the rest of the territory is freezing out, we're having a mild winter. But nobody ever laid claim to the Sweetwater Valley because the big cowmen knew it would start a range war. But now that Ella and I have taken a pair of quarter sections here under the Homestead Act, Reese Clarke is worried that other folks might get the same idea. So that's why he comes around here trying to scare us off. If there isn't a law that'll run us out of here, then he's determined to make one up to suit him."

Ella said, "But he won't go to court because he doesn't have a case."

Chase Malone nodded. "That's right. All he can do is what he did when he was here — call us names. Last winter he called us outlaws and cattle thieves. He threatened to bring the sheriff up here to look at the bill of sale for our stock. He said a rep from the Stockgrowers' Association would be out here any day. Nobody ever showed. Now, he's calling us trespassers and gamblers. A few months from now it will be something else."

"He's already called me something else," Ella mumbled.

"Boomer, I'd give anything to be your

age," Chase Malone went on. "This territory is getting settled up more every year. It will go fast from now on. You'll live to see more changes than I ever will. I first came through this valley on an army patrol. We were chasing a band of Cheyenne led by White Wolf." He laughed. "We never caught him. But from that day to this, I've believed the Sweetwater Valley was a natural place for a settlement of small ranches and farms and a village. The railroad hits Sunbonnet thirty miles south of here. If there is ever a big north-south rail line, it will likely come through here. And if it does, you can bet this little valley will grow faster than mushrooms after rain."

Ella said dreamily, "Do you really think that will happen, Chase?"

"No man knows what the future will bring," Chase Malone said. "But like I was saying, Boomer, if you stay in these parts, you'll see what happens and you'll be a part of it."

"We all will," Ella said.

I was caught up in Chase Malone's vision of the future. I'd never heard anyone talk about it the way he had. Back home my father spoke of the future as something to fear. The future brought changes, and changes were usually bad. But Chase Malone excited me with his talk about my having a stake in the future and about all of us benefitting from the settlement of the land.

Suddenly, I wanted to go outside to look at the valley, as though I would be able to see the ghosts of the future. Ella and Chase Malone had fallen silent and after a time I got up and went out.

The sun was down, but the blue and cloudless sky was still sunlit. Birds had begun singing their evening songs in the cottonwoods. I led my pony around the yard in front of Chase Malone's saloon, breathing in the fragrant air of the Sweetwater Valley and thinking of the future. I didn't see any ghosts.

When Ella came out of the saloon, she was smiling and flushed. Chase Malone stood on the porch and waved goodbye as we walked to the wagon ruts that ran through the tall grass. In silence we followed the ruts to the cabin, the pony clomping along behind us, keeping slack in the lead rope.

It was after dark by the time we finished cleaning up the dinner dishes. Ella said we were eating like rich folks. They didn't have to clean up after themselves so they never worried about eating late. I was too tired and groggy to think straight by that time. I lit a lantern and said good night to her.

I stopped at the corral long enough to have a last look at my pony. When I had turned him into the corral that evening, he had made a big show of prancing around and kicking up his heels. Billy and Bobby had stood together and watched him sleepily. Now when I raised the lantern I saw the three horses standing close together at the far end of the corral.

Happy that he had made peace with them, I went into the barn. After I had blown out the lantern and crawled in the bunk, I heard an owl.

"Whoo! Whoo!"

I thought, "Me! Me!"

I was almost asleep when I heard noises in the yard. One of the horses in the corral whinnied. I looked out through a crack between the boards, half expecting to see the cowboy named Buck Stone.

But by the light from the cabin door I saw Chase Malone. He went inside and Ella closed the door behind him, leaving the yard in darkness again.

CHAPTER VI

Ella was in a silly mood in the morning. She giggled and chattered all through breakfast. I wondered what had happened to make her act that way. I ate a big breakfast of flapjacks, sowbelly, and biscuits without saying any more than I had to because every time I did say anything Ella started giggling again.

But after we had finished cleaning up the breakfast dishes I found out what was on Ella's mind.

"I dreamed of that pony of yours," she said.

"You did?"

She nodded excitedly. "Have you figured out what you're going to do with him?"

"No," I admitted. "But I'm keeping him."

"Oh, don't worry," she said, "I won't try to talk you out of keeping him. I mean, have you decided what you're going to do with him in case some Indian comes looking for him?"

I had been trying not to think about it. "I guess I could find a place to hide him.

Maybe I could put him back in the trees somewhere."

"But you can't hide him all the time, can you?" Ella asked. "Sometime you'll have to bring him out to graze, won't you?" Ella giggled as though she was coming to the end of a joke. "I dreamed of a way to keep anybody from finding him."

"You did?"

"You go out to the corral and catch him and snub him to a post. Snub him tight. I'll be right out."

"What are you going to do," I asked, "cut his head off?"

Ella laughed. "How did you guess?"

When I got to the corral, the pony must have thought I had something for him to eat because he walked right up to me and searched me with his nose. He looked surprised when I threw a rope on him and snubbed him down. He gave me a look that said, "Boy, I'll never trust you again."

Ella came out of the cabin carrying a fancy traveling case of some kind. I guessed that was what it was, anyway. It was too big to be a purse. The case was shiny black with pictures of gaudy women painted on the sides. She set it on the corner of the stock trough and opened it. I took a close look at the pictures because some of the women didn't have much on. The case was full of little round jars and metal containers and funny-looking brushes.

"Were you an actress?" I asked.

"You might say that," she said, as she opened up containers of pink, red, and orange make-up. When she found what she was looking for, she took a soft cloth and began smearing a dull shade of red on my pony's white face.

"What are you doing?" I asked.

The pony must have wondered the same thing because he shook his head in protest and kicked up a storm of dust. Ella cooed at him as she worked. After a while the pony quieted and cocked his notched ears at us.

"Turn him loose, Boomer."

When I untied the rope, the pony watched us for half a second, then leaped away toward the center of the corral like he had just stuck his head inside a beehive. I could hardly believe what I was seeing. He was a pure roan pony now, without a trace of white on his head.

Ella laughed. "My dream's come true, Boomer!"

"He doesn't even look like my pony."

"I don't reckon any Indian would recognize him now," Ella said. "Not from a distance, anyway. Up close, those ears are a give-away. But anybody who's hunting a whiteheaded horse wouldn't give this one a second look."

"How long will that make-up last?"

"I don't know," Ella said. "But I've known women who've kept the same make-up on for four or five days. It should stay on that long if he doesn't try to rub it off. But when some white begins to show, I'll put on some more. If we can keep him disguised for two or three weeks, I think our worries will be over."

The pony pranced around the circle of the corral. He had forgotten about shaking his head and now he was showing off. He bucked a few times, then ran around the corral, kicking up clods of manure. Ella's two geldings stood close together and watched patiently.

I felt Ella watching me. "What are you thinking, Boomer?"

"Even with a red head," I said, "he's beautiful."

Ella reached over and ran her hand through my hair in a rough way. "I kind of thought that was what was on your mind. Why don't you catch him again and take him out and graze him. Let old Billy and Bobby out, too. They won't go far, but keep an eye on them, anyway. I don't have a south fence yet. If something should spook them, they might run from here to the railroad."

I told Ella that I wanted to ride the pony.

"You might wait on that," she said, looking in the corral. "White Wolf had him gentled for a saddle, but that don't mean he's saddle-broke. I don't know much about gentling horses, but I'd say go easy with him at first. Let him get to know who you are. He seems like a good-natured pony, but he's still pretty wild."

I spent the rest of the morning and the whole afternoon with the pony. I led him out to the tall grass and talked to him and petted him while he grazed. In the afternoon I spent a good deal of time currying him. Billy and Bobby wandered out through the yard into the grass. They grazed for a while, then they would go down and roll, grunting and groaning with the pleasure. My pony got better treatment. I curried him until his deep red coat shone in the afternoon sunlight like a ruby.

Three days passed quickly and in much the same way. I did chores around the place and tended the horses, paying particular attention to my pony. On the third day I was able to sit on him bareback while he grazed. Each day I expected White Wolf to come to the cabin and see how I was getting along with the pony, but he never did. As it worked out, I went to see him.

I had the horses out to graze, but I hadn't realized anything was wrong until Ella stepped out of the cabin, looked from the corral to where I stood with the pony, and called, "Boomer, where's Billy and Bobby?"

I turned around and my heart purely froze when I saw they were gone. I ran out toward the wagon ruts so I could look up and down the valley.

Ella shouted after me, "Hunt for them down the valley. Don't go north. There's a good fence up there to stop them. Watch out for rattlers!"

Billy and Bobby hadn't wandered far. I ran down the wagon ruts for a quarter of a mile when I saw them standing in the high grass between the ruts and the tree line. They watched me as I circled behind them. But before I had a chance to begin shooing them up the road, they both took off at a trot back up the valley. Then they broke into a gallop. I stopped and watched them pound up toward the cabin.

"You stupid plugs," I said, but I knew they were making me look stupid. The two geldings would be waiting for me at the corral. If they could talk, they would ask me what took me so long to get back home. I picked up an egg-shaped stone and threw it after them. Then I picked up another and threw it into the trees by the river.

That was how I saw a haze of smoke drifting out of the cottonwoods. Instinctively, I dropped into the grass. I watched, but saw nothing in the shadows of the cottonwood grove. I thought of running back up to the cabin to tell Ella she had trespassers, but then I remembered White Wolf.

I looked up the valley toward the cabin. Billy and Bobby were long gone. They were probably at the stock trough by now.

I studied the tree line below the haze of smoke. In the shadows I saw no movement. I remembered reading in a library book that it was almost impossible for a white man to sneak up on an encampment of Indians without being seen. Indians could sneak up on white men, but whites could never sneak up on Indians. It was one of the unexplained mysteries of life in the West, the book said. The book had been written by an explorer, but I couldn't remember which one. All I remembered was that as I read it, I believed that I was one of the few whites who could sneak up on an Indian camp without being seen. All I needed was a chance to prove it.

I kept low and moved through the grassy field to the tree line where I lunged into the cool shade of the cottonwood grove a hundred or so yards above the haze of smoke. I stepped carefully and quietly through the sparse underbrush, taking slow steps and easing my weight down on each foot as I moved through the trees. The air was so still that my breathing seemed as loud as a wind.

Closer to the Sweetwater River bank the underbrush was much thicker and would have made a better screen. But it was too dense and tangled to get through. By staying near the edge of the grove I could move faster. I came on to what looked like a growth of brush, but then I saw horses and realized it was a makeshift corral. The excitement of the discovery made my heart pound like a drum.

The corral was so cleverly built that as I was walking around it, I knew if I hadn't seen the spotted horses inside, I wouldn't have recognized it for what it was. I came around the corral and saw the smoky fire. I suddenly realized the shape between the fire and the corral was a white-haired squaw. She wore a long, shapeless buckskin dress as she squatted before the fire, putting green branches on it.

Something soft and strong hit me from behind. A bare arm came around my neck and pulled back against my throat. Hot, fierce breath blew against the side of my face and a pair of strong legs gripped my sides as I was ridden down to the cool earth.

I couldn't breathe. A wild roar filled my ears. I struggled and finally tore the tightened arm from my throat and rolled over on my back. A murderous shriek cut the air as I looked up to see an Indian girl sitting on top of me. She waved a knife over her head, her mouth torn open by long, terrifying shrieks.

My shoulders were pinned to the ground by her knees. I fought, but couldn't throw her off. Every move I made only brought more screams from her as she slashed the air above my face with the knife. I tried to raise my arms far enough to get a hold on her waist, but I couldn't reach that far. I tried to grasp her hips and shove her away. All I managed to do was to shove her buckskin dress farther up her legs. I tried for another grip and shoved again.

The girl stopped in the middle of a long shriek and stared down at me in surprise. The shining knife that had been flashing overhead now hung over me as though frozen in the air. I heard guttural voices. The Indian girl must have heard them, too. She sucked in a long breath of air and began screaming again. The white-haired squaw stood over us. Then White Wolf was beside her. He yanked the girl off me and sent her sprawling. The knife flew up into the air, fell to the earth, and slid into the underbrush like a gleaming snake.

White Wolf laughed as he pulled me to my feet. He spoke, but I couldn't understand him. My legs were weak and my heart raced like a steam engine. I had struggled hard enough to bring the taste of blood to my mouth.

White Wolf led me past the smoky campfire and around the corral. We followed a wandering path through the trees, a path that almost doubled back on itself before reaching the river. White Wolf led me through brush so thick that I lost any trace of a path. Willows slapped at me as I followed. The smell of the grove and the river filled my nose.

Then we broke into a small clearing that opened onto the riverbank like a room.

Two tepees stood close together in the clearing. White Wolf threw open the flap of a tepee marked with a red circle that I took to be a symbol for the sun. He motioned for me to follow him inside.

I must have hesitated for he said, "I am White Wolf. You sit at my fire."

When I ducked into the near darkness inside the tepee, I was surprised to see a small fire burning in the center. I had seen no smoke coming out of the tepee, yet the fire back at the corral was as smoky as any I'd ever seen. White Wolf sat on one of the furry hides scattered around the fire, and motioned for me to sit on one across from him.

"Sit at my fire," he said again. "Welcome."

The tepee smelled of smoke, leather, and humans. Those smells that became mixed into one, took my memory back to the first time I'd seen White Wolf, the time he'd given me water and I'd feared him and tried to escape. Now I watched him light his Scottish pipe from a blazing twig, cross his legs before him, and sigh with contentment. I guessed he had been sitting in this way when he had heard the girl scream.

White Wolf said nothing as he smoked. He watched the little fire, stirring it now and then. Once when he glanced at me, I smiled at him. He nodded. I thought of telling him about the pony. But I couldn't think of an easy way to explain it. And I wondered how he would take it if he did know. He might be offended.

We must have sat there for nearly half an hour. The taste of blood had gone out of my mouth and my heart had stopped trying to leap out of my chest. When I let my eyes close I no longer saw the nightmare of the knife slashing over me, the blade coming down. With the warmth of the tepee and the soft hide inviting me, I shifted my legs until I lay on my side, facing the fire. Then my head rested in soft fur and the low, crackling sounds of the fire grew far away. I didn't fear White Wolf. He wasn't a savage any more.

The sharp laughter of women woke me. White Wolf grunted unhappily. I sat up and rubbed my eyes. I thought I'd recognized one of the voices, but at the same time I wondered if I'd dreamed it.

The tepee flap was thrown open and Ella's head poked through. "What the hell you doing here, Boomer?"

"I was just talking to White Wolf," I said.

"Well, you sure gave me a scare. Billy and Bobby came back to the corral, but you never showed up." She looked at White Wolf. "So you decided to go visiting. Howdy, White Wolf."

He nodded at her. I got up and stepped outside.

Ella had a crooked smile on her face when she asked, "What did you do to this little Indian girl, Boomer? She's been working hard to make me understand how bad she hates you."

The white-haired squaw and two younger squaws stood in the clearing outside the tepee. The girl crouched behind the old squaw, half hiding. We looked at each other, then she turned and ran up the path that led to the corral.

"She's that crazy Birdy that Chase Malone told us about," I said. "I didn't do anything to her."

"She probably hates you because you're so handsome," Ella said.

When White Wolf came out of the tepee, he wore a big buffalo robe over his shoulders. I said goodbye to him and we shook hands. I suddenly wondered how old he was. His eyelids drooped over his black eyes and his face sagged away from the high and wide cheekbones, making deep lines on each side of his Cheyenne nose. After Ella and I had left White Wolf's camp and were walking along the wagon ruts on our way back to the cabin, I asked her how old White Wolf was.

She shook her head. "I couldn't even guess. Why?"

"He looked so tired," I said. "And old."

Ella came closer and put her arm around my shoulders. "If you had that many women in your life, Boomer, you'd be tired, too."

I felt too embarrassed to look at her. My memory shot back to the Indian girl sitting on top of me and what I had seen.

Ella tightened her grip on my shoulders. "You can be mighty glad you have only one woman in your life, Boomer Jones. And I'm not letting anybody take you away from me."

CHAPTER VII

In the early afternoon of the next day Chase Malone rode into the yard on that same plunging, wild-eyed horse he had been on the first time I ever saw him.

I was down at the corral. When Chase Malone dismounted and tied his big horse to the tie post in front of the cabin, yanking a solid knot as he did so, Ella came outside. I saw them standing together, talking, and I thought Ella might be telling him about my pony.

But when I walked toward them I saw that Chase Malone was doing the talking. I heard him, I mean. His voice boomed like it had that time he had ridden into the yard and cussed Ella for carrying on with Buck Stone. Chase Malone clenched a folded newspaper in his hand. As he talked, he waved it like he was swatting horseflies. I wasn't surprised to hear Buck Stone's name.

"You mean Buck didn't come down here?" Chase Malone asked. "He was up at my place just this morning."

Ella shook her head.

"I can't figure that," Chase Malone said, but I could tell he was pleased by the idea when he turned to greet me.

Ella said, "Buck probably has too many other women friends in the territory to be stopping by here every week."

Chase Malone grinned. "Well, I don't."

"I know," Ella said. "You ain't as eligible."

"Now, goddammit, Ella —"

"Just what did Buck tell you?" Ella asked. Then she looked at me. "Wait. You two come on inside. We might as well hear this over coffee."

We sat around the rough pine table as Chase Malone opened the newspaper and thrust it toward Ella. She didn't take it. Chase Malone stared at her for a full half minute, then jerked the paper back and held it to the light that streamed in from the open doorway.

"Well, I'll read you a letter that was written to the editor of the Sunbonnet *Global News* —"

Ella broke in, "Somebody wrote a letter to Cotton Turner?"

"Not exactly," Chase Malone said. "It's written to everybody, but it was sent to Cotton Turner so he could publish it."

"Who wrote it?"

"Reese Clarke."

"He did?" Ella asked. "Well, how did you get hold of that paper? Did you sneak into town?"

"Why, hell no," Chase Malone said. "Buck Stone brought it by this morning."

"Oh, so that's why you were asking about him," Ella said. "Well, what does Reese Clarke say in that letter?"

"I'm going to read it if you'll let me get to it," Chase Malone said.

"Go right ahead," Ella said pleasantly.

Chase Malone cleared his throat. " 'Editor: In the interest of Democracy and True Justice, I must bring to the attention of all the good Citizens of the entire Territory of Wyoming another criminal outrage. Outlaws and thieves of all descriptions have long plagued Civilization. We here in the great Territory of Wyoming are by no means exempt from threats by unsavory Characters who lurk in our unpopulated regions. These Characters thirst for the wealth and very blood of the hardworking and honest Populace. Our good Sheriff and his fine Deputies are overextended. There is far too much land in the county for but a few hardy Men to police. The sad result is that Criminals of all descriptions have numerous lairs. I personally believe the benefits of Statehood will solve many problems of this category. However, that happy Event is yet to come. Our problem, of course, is what to do now.

" 'I call your attention to the Sweetwater Valley. It is common knowledge that for the past two decades I personally have used this uninhabited valley for winter range. I have hardly been alone in this practice. Other cowmen of the region such as Matthew Morganthau, R. A. Tingley, Harold Hamlyn, and others have benefitted from the native grasslands of the Sweetwater Valley for years. In the grip of hard winters this practice has doubtless saved many head of Stock. Stockgrowing is, as is generally known, the very backbone of the Territory's Economy.

" 'But now the Sweetwater Valley has been taken over by certain ruthless, unsavory Characters. I will not set their names in writing as I believe that no one knows their True Names. No matter: we know who they are. We know they have, with no Prior Right whatsoever, cut the very heart from the Sweetwater Valley, thrown fences up, and taken it for themselves. You may ask, Who are these greedy Persons who must live in a remote valley out of the reach of Civilization and out of the grasp of our Laws? One man is a former soldier, cashiered into early retirement, who now deals in the sale of hard liquors. It is commonly said that he has killed his man. One can only believe his Patrons must be either Indians or White Men who ride what is generally known as the Owlhoot Trail. If not, why would they go to such uncomfortable extremes to avoid Civilization? Another newcomer to the Sweetwater Valley is an unsavory woman who presently resides in the dirt and filth and stench of a Wolfer's ancient shack. I shall only mention that her identity, if not her True Name, is well known to the Sheriff of Sunbonnet.

" 'As I stated at the beginning, I have asked Officers of the Law to investigate this ruthless Criminal seizure of public lands. I have no doubts that our duly elected Officials will do all within their power to uphold the Laws of the Land. However, I personally recognize and shall not neglect my duty to the honest Citizens of Wyoming Territory in this year of 1889 and hearby inform them in specific detail of this newest Criminal activity in our land. No cost will be too great to invest in stopping these ruthless Trespassers; nor will any action be too drastic. Reese Clarke C Bar Ranch.' "

Ella asked, "Was that us he was writing about?"

"Sure, it's us," Chase Malone said.

"What was that he was saying about me?"

"I just read it to you, Ella. Didn't you hear?"

"I heard it," Ella said, "but he had so many words in there that I lost track of what he was getting at. What does 'unsavory' mean, anyway?"

Chase Malone smiled. "When he was writing about you, he meant that you're not exactly innocent."

"Thank God for that," she said. "It's the innocent girls in this world who get hurt."

"I don't think that's how he meant it."

"He wasn't calling me a whore, was he?"

Chase Malone hesitated. "No, he didn't say that. But he did claim you can't keep house."

"You mean that business about the wolfer's shack?" Ella asked. "How would he know? He's never been in there since we got the place cleaned up."

"I don't believe Reese Clarke was interested in writing the truth," Chase Malone said.

"Sounds to me like he's a little moon-struck these days," Ella said.

Chase Malone leaned back in the chair. "It was his same old song. He claims I'm doing whiskey business with Indians and outlaws."

Ella laughed. "What he means is, you're doing business with C Bar riders."

Chase Malone began to look irritated with Ella. "You're missing the point, Ella. Clarke wants folks to believe the worst about us. He wants folks to think we're harboring a bunch of outlaws up here, that we're dealing in whiskey-selling and prostitution, and that we don't even have a legal claim to be here."

"But why?" Ella asked. "What do I care what those people in Sunbonnet believe. They already believe the worst about me."

"Some do and some don't, Ella," Chase Malone said. "But if Reese Clarke can get enough folks believing those things he wrote, then he can make trouble for us. He's a respected man in the territory. He's been a member of the Stockgrowers' Association for twenty-some years."

Ella snorted. "What's so goddam respectable about that? Most of those old boys are the biggest cattle thieves and land grabbers in the whole territory."

114

"Maybe so," Chase Malone said. "But Reese Clarke is a man who can use public opinion to try us and judge us. If his plan works, then he can find us guilty and run us out of the territory without any of the good citizens lifting a finger to stop him."

"He'll have his hands full," Ella said. "When you talk about those respected men who go down to the Cheyenne Club and have their little business meetings and so on, my temperature goes up. I know better. I've seen these respected ranchers that ride into Cheyenne two or three times a year. Oh, they're family and churchgoing men when they're at home. But let them get down there in the Cheyenne Club, and you wouldn't know them. Believe me, you wouldn't know them."

"Those are the men who have power in this territory," Chase Malone said.

Ella shrugged. "When the day comes for a dude like Reese Clarke to run me off my land, that will be a day he won't soon forget. And don't tell me you're just going to pack up and pull out."

"I hope it doesn't come to that point," Chase Malone said.

"What do you aim to do?"

"I'll draft a letter of my own to be published in the newspaper," Chase Malone said. "Maybe I can head off some wrong ideas that Reese Clarke is trying to plant. That's one reason I came down here. I'm going to town tomorrow to hand the letter to Cotton Turner. You want me to pick up any supplies for you?"

"Chase Malone, I haven't been to town since fall. I'm not about to let you sneak off and whoop it up while me and Boomer are working our fingers to the bone up here in the valley."

"I didn't think you'd want to go back since you had the trouble," Chase Malone said.

"The almighty town council can ban me from Sunbonnet maybe, but they can't ban me from Saloon Row. Coralee wouldn't put up with it."

Chase Malone laughed. "No, she probably wouldn't for a fact."

"Besides," Ella said, "the hired hand needs to be outfitted. And if I don't go to town with you, you'll forget to buy the fencing. You promised to put in my south fence as soon as winter broke."

Chase Malone grimaced. "So I did. Well, it'll be easier now that we got a hired man working for us." He looked at me. "By the way, why isn't this man out working instead of sitting in here with us land owners?"

"He's been slaving since sunup, Chase," Ella said. "That reminds me, Boomer, did you tell him about your pony?"

They both laughed when I said I hadn't been able to get a word in edgewise. After I'd told Chase Malone about the pony, he said:

"I'll have to see this."

My pony was inside the corral with Billy and Bobby. His coat was shining and I felt proud of him as he alertly watched us walk toward the corral. The color on his face was still a close match to the rest of his body. He tossed his head and snorted at me, then came a few steps closer.

"Ella, you missed your calling," Chase Malone said. "You should have been a horse trader. An unprincipled woman like you could take a jackass, trim his ears down, paint him yellow, and sell him for a palomino."

"Unprincipled," Ella said. "Is that anything like unsavory?"

"Worse," Chase Malone said.

"Do you think I ought to take such talk off him, Boomer?"

I looked at them as they stood leaning on the top pole of the corral. I'd never heard a grown man and woman talk to each other the way they did. They acted like they were fighting one minute, but then the next minute they acted like they were in love and they should be married.

"Don't ask him," Chase Malone said. "All he can think about is that keg-footed Indian pony out there."

"He's not keg-footed," I said. Both Ella and Chase Malone laughed then.

As we walked back toward Chase Malone's horse, Ella asked him if he wanted to stay for supper.

"I'd like to, Ella, but if I'm going to get that letter worked out, I'd better get on home and do it."

"Well, you come on down for breakfast, anyway," Ella said.

He nodded. "I'll be here at first light. We need to start by sunup or before."

We watched him ride off. His big horse tried to walk sideways for a while before Chase Malone got him straightened around. We went into the cabin and I heard Ella say something about a bank.

"What?" I asked.

"I'll have to make a withdrawal from the bank," she said.

I nodded, wondering why she was telling me about going to the bank tomorrow. But then she dragged the kindling box away from the stove and with her gardening trowel she dug into the dirt floor. The dirt was mixed with ashes and was not packed hard. After she had dug down six or eight inches the trowel scraped against metal. I watched her smooth the dirt away and pull out a steel box. She brought out a key from a chain around her neck and opened the box.

I didn't know how much money was inside, but I could see right away there was much more there than the five hundred dollars my father kept beneath his bed. Ella took out several bills, closed up the box, and set it back in the hole. After she had covered it I helped her drag the box of stove wood back up against the iron stove.

Ella left the money on the kitchen table. She started to say something to me, but then she turned away and started building up the fire in the stove. I went outside while she was busy getting supper together. I stayed at the corral with my pony until she called me. All during supper I knew something was on her mind, but she didn't say anything until we were through eating.

"Boomer, I've been looking for the right words to tell you this, but I can't come up with much. I have to tell you that you're the only other person on this earth besides me who knows where I keep my money. Not even Chase Malone knows. I don't know why I haven't told him. I guess I'm afraid it would ruin something . . . some feeling we have between us. I can't find the words for that, either. But it seems right for you to know. And I want to tell you that if anything ever happens to me, that money is yours. I want you to come and dig it up if anything . . . I don't want any of my relatives to have it. They wouldn't approve of what I did to earn it. Chase Malone doesn't need it. You're the one I want to have it."

I was confused and embarrassed. "Nothing's going to happen to you."

She smiled. "That's right, Boomer — unless I get bit by a rattler or hit by lightning."

I felt relieved. I knew nothing like that would happen to her.

CHAPTER VIII

When Ella woke me the morning was still dark and quiet. I thought I had been under the blankets only a few minutes.

Ella rustled my hair. "Don't go back to sleep on me. Get your clothes on and come up for breakfast."

I dressed by the light of the lantern Ella had left. Outside, in the early morning darkness, the smell of wood smoke filled the air. I hooked the lantern on a nail in a corral post above the stock trough. I rinsed my face and swallowed some of the cold water. As I wiped my face against my sleeves, I looked up and saw my pony inside the corral. He stood close to Billy and Bobby, watching me.

Chase Malone's big saddle horse was tied at the rack in front of the cabin. When I came up alongside him, he tried to rear away from me. I told him to settle down, but he only snorted and rolled his eyes as though he thought I was going to kill him.

When I opened the cabin door, the smell of breakfast hit me. Chase Malone sat at the table before a steaming cup of coffee. He greeted me and Ella half turned from the stove and told me I was just in time. She served up the breakfast and we ate in silence. None of us was awake enough to say much.

By the time Chase Malone and I had Billy and Bobby hooked up to the buckboard, it was light enough to see. We were ready to go, but Ella was still inside the cabin.

"How long does it take that woman to fix herself?" Chase Malone grumbled. "Ella! Let's go! *Elllaaa!*"

After a few minutes she came out, wearing a long duster and a bonnet. I helped her into the wagon seat and climbed up after her. By the time we turned down the valley to follow the wagon ruts southward, the pale sky was shot with streaks of pink and orange. The valley was still in shadow and smelled of dew.

Before reaching White Wolf's camp we saw a herd of deer coming out of the cottonwoods after a morning drink. The lead bucks stopped along the edge of the tree line and watched us pass by. Back in the trees I saw several does, standing as still as statues.

We had gone a short distance farther

when Ella said, "White Wolf's camp is back in there somewhere."

Chase Malone nodded as he looked into the trees. Then he glanced at me. "I hear you camped with White Wolf yesterday."

As soon as he mentioned it, all I could think of was that Indian girl.

"How many women did he have with him?" Chase Malone asked.

"Three that I saw," I said.

"Four with that little girl," Ella added.

"Birdy is usually with him," Chase Malone said.

"She hates Boomer," Ella said, glancing at me with a smile.

"Why's that?" Chase Malone asked.

Ella looked at me. "I don't know," I said.

"She hates him because he's so handsome," Ella said.

"That's all the reason that loco girl needs," Chase Malone said. Then he added, "In years past I've seen six or eight women in White Wolf's camp, all of them waiting on him hand and foot."

"Why so many?" I asked.

Chase Malone shrugged. "For some reason a Cheyenne squaw would sooner run off with him than anybody. I don't know what he's got, but it sure works — whatever it is. He's supposed to be in disgrace with the whole Cheyenne nation, but that doesn't keep the women away from him. What's that man got, Ella?"

Ella said she didn't know.

Chase Malone tried to whisper around her, "I'm glad she doesn't."

Ella let it go without saying anything. I found myself wanting to know more about the Indian girl, but I didn't know how to ask without them suspecting something. Instead I told Chase Malone about the brush corral and the smoky fire.

"Was it a cookfire?" he asked.

"I didn't see any pots around the fire," I said. "It was far away from the tepees. All I saw was an old squaw putting green willow branches on it."

Ella said, "There was hardly a trail at all between the fire and the tepees, Chase. It wound back through the brush for forty, fifty yards. I never would have found Boomer if the women hadn't taken me back there."

Chase Malone nodded thoughtfully. The wagon passed by a bunch of cattle. They shied away from the wagon like wild animals. Ella asked Chase Malone what he made of White Wolf's strange camp.

"An Indian won't build a fire without a reason," he said. "Since he's keeping up a smoky fire, I'd say he is trying to let every-body know where he is. That isn't like White Wolf."

"Then why is he doing it?" Ella asked when he had grown silent.

"My guess is that fire by the corral is a decoy," Chase Malone said. "He's expect-ing some unfriendly company."

"Who?" I asked, even though I thought I knew.

"The owner of that little whiteheaded pony, most likely."

Ella smiled at me. "He won't find one in these parts, will he?"

"Nope," Chase Malone laughed, "he sure won't."

But I wasn't so sure. I wished we'd tied the pony on the tailgate and brought him with us. Then I wouldn't have to worry about whether he would be in the corral when we got back. Ella asked Chase Malone how the fire would work as a decoy.

He pushed his hat back on his head and leaned forward with his elbows on his knees. "The way I see it, White Wolf knows a brave will be coming after that horse. It won't take long for the brave to guess that White Wolf is holed up here on the Sweetwater. When that happens, the brave will want to come bellying into camp, put a gun to his ear or a knife to his throat, and ask for the return of his top war horse. About all White Wolf can do is claim he doesn't know a thing about his horse and hope for mercy. He may get it and he may not. Probably not since the brave knows that White Wolf is one of the few Indians who would know how to get away with such a prize horse. So White Wolf has set up a decoy camp for the brave to sneak into. He'll find the fire and the corral and maybe a couple of the women. Maybe the brave will take what's in the corral and leave. Or maybe he'll figure out what White Wolf's done and start poking around in the brush. But if he does, he'll give White Wolf enough of a warning that he'll have time to fight back or get away."

"White Wolf is one smart Indian," Ella said. "You can see why he was chief for so many years."

Chase Malone nodded. "The Cheyenne made a mistake when they threw him away from the tribe for killing Starved Bear. But, hell, they have their laws just like we do. I reckon they have to stick by them."

We came on to some more cattle farther down the valley. They raised their heads

126

from grazing and watched us. A few skittered away.

Chase Malone said, "Seeing how jumpy the stock is, I'd guess old One Eye isn't far off."

"I wonder where," Ella asked.

"Back up in one of those draws, likely," Chase Malone said, pointing toward the red cliffs. "Off by himself like the devil."

"Maybe he is the devil," Ella said.

"Who's he coming for?" he asked. "You or me?"

"Who's One Eye?" I asked.

Chase Malone said, "Oh, he's an old red steer with one eye poked out, loco as a fish on a bank. He belongs to Ella."

"No, he doesn't," Ella said. "He's usually up on your claim, Chase, along with that wild horse of yours. All of them drink Malone's whiskey, Boomer."

Chase Malone didn't rise to that bait.

Ella explained to me. "One Eye wandered into the valley last winter. At least, that was the first time we saw him. I believe he runs from one end of the Sweetwater to the other. We've never got close enough to him to read his brand. It looks to be covered over with matted hair, anyway. No telling where he came from. Whoever owned him was probably glad to

127

see him run off. He's not good for anything."

"Except spooking the other cattle," Chase Malone said. Then he added, "I'd try to shoot him, but I'm afraid he'd catch the bullet in his teeth and throw it back at me."

Ella laughed. I asked what made the steer loco.

"Losing that one eye might have done it," Chase Malone said. "Or he might have eaten some loco weed."

Ella nudged me in the ribs. "Chase, are you sure he didn't get into some of the whiskey you made up?"

A sour look twisted his mouth. "I wouldn't waste it on a steer."

"Unless he could pay," Ella said.

Chase Malone yanked his hat low on his forehead, but said nothing.

Ella jabbed my ribs with her elbow again. "What's the recipe for that whiskey of yours?"

"I can't tell you," Chase Malone muttered.

"Why not?"

"It's a family secret."

"If you had a family," Ella asked, "then why would Reese Clarke call you a bastard?"

"Careful, woman."

Ella nudged me. "One part whiskey to

128

ten parts water."

Chase Malone ignored her and stared ahead in silence, holding the reins in his hands. The red cliffs broke up and seemed to fall away as the Sweetwater Valley opened into the desert. The cottonwood grove grew sparse. The river took a turn and we crossed it and climbed out of the valley through a break in the rocks.

We were in the desert. It was broken country like the desert I had gotten lost in, with nothing to see but stunted sagebrush, brown sticker weeds, and low curled grass. The twin wagon ruts stretched across the desert like a pair of thin snakes.

Ella started in on Chase Malone again: "How many plugs of tobacco goes into that whiskey of yours?"

Chase Malone spoke without looking at her. "Don't rile me, woman."

"What do you aim to do to stop me?"

Chase Malone didn't answer.

"Can't hear you," she said.

"You'll be walking to Sunbonnet," Chase Malone said at last.

Ella snorted. "You don't think you're man enough to throw me off this wagon seat, do you?"

"Hell, yes."

"I hear plenty of big talk," Ella said,

poking me in the ribs, "but I don't see no action."

At first I thought Chase Malone was going to let that go by, too. He sat still and looked ahead where there was nothing to see. Then he passed the reins over to me and in one quick motion circled his arms around Ella. She shrieked with laughter. Chase Malone shouted that he was going to squeeze her to death, then throw her carcass into a manure pile where it belonged. When she struggled against his grip, I felt her bumping against me. Billy and Bobby perked up and looked back to see what was going on. They slowed and stopped.

Ella had laughed herself out of breath by the time Chase Malone turned loose. Her bonnet was cockeyed on her head and strands of hair had fallen in front of her face.

Chase Malone adjusted his sleeves and took the reins back. "I told you not to rile me," he said, slapping the reins against the team's rumps.

It took a while for Ella to get her breath back. She took off her bonnet, straightened her hair, and put it back on. "That's the worst unsavory beating I ever had," she said. She laughed again and put her arm

130

around my shoulders. "What are you thinking, Boomer?"

I said, "I don't think One Eye is the only loco one in the valley."

Ella and Chase Malone roared with laughter. Chase Malone slapped his hand on his knee and stomped his boots up and down on the floorboards. Ella wiped tears from her eyes.

No one said much for a long time. I looked back and was surprised that I could hardly see a trace of the red rocks and cliffs that marked the Sweetwater Valley. It was as though the land had closed up and swallowed the place. I felt a sense of emptiness, as though the desert had pressed its silence down on us like a lid.

We saw a few jackrabbits and several small herds of antelope. The antelope watched us, but unlike the deer in the valley, they were curious and would often walk toward us several steps. Chase Malone said that we must look like a strange animal with four wheels instead of legs.

Billy and Bobby were a good wagon team. By the time the sun was high and turning the air warm, the two geldings were keeping the same pace they had started out with. It wasn't a fast pace, but it wasn't slow, either. It was a pace that ate up the miles, and Billy and Bobby acted like they could keep it up all day.

Later in the morning we were in sight of a low range of mountains. On the horizon ahead they were blue and purple, stabbing sharply toward wisps of stringy clouds in the sky.

"Sunbonnet," Ella said.

I thought it was a funny name for a town. I asked how it came to be named Sunbonnet.

"You'll see," Ella said.

And in another half an hour I did. A strange rock formation sat off to the right. It was made up of huge rounded boulders, but one that was larger than the others had one side broken off and in the distance it did look something like a sunbonnet.

"That's a signature rock," Chase Malone said. "The pioneers and gold seekers who came through here in the old days stopped near that rock for water."

I had read about signature rocks in library books. Pioneers carved their names in them and the date they had come there.

"Where does the water come from?" I asked.

Chase Malone said, "This is the lower end of the Sweetwater, Boomer. After it leaves the valley the river wanders through the desert and comes out down here. The town of Sunbonnet is about five miles south of the old signature rock. When we cross the river there, you won't recognize it. It's shallow and wide."

"I wonder what those pioneers would have thought if they knew how close they were to a pretty little valley like the Sweetwater?" Ella said.

"A lot of them never would have gone on to Oregon," Chase Malone said.

"Couldn't they have followed these wagon ruts up to the valley?" I asked.

Chase Malone said, "This is an old army road, Boomer. It goes back a few years, but not that far."

"It's a shortcut," Ella said.

"That's right," Chase Malone said. "The way the river wanders around, you'd spend weeks trying to follow it back to the valley."

"How did anybody find the valley?"

Chase Malone said, "Oh, trappers and wolfers who spent their lives following rivers have known about it. But those men weren't the kind who would make a point of telling folks about the place. A trapper might think the Sweetwater Valley would be a good place for him to settle in one day. The cabin Ella lives in was probably built by a trapper forty, fifty years back."

"Did a trapper build it for his home?" I asked.

"It's hard to say," Chase Malone said. "It's been empty since the first time I came through this country with the Army. A trapper might have hurt himself late in the year and maybe he and his partner had to build it to keep the weather off them. Or the Indians might have run off the animals from a couple of fur trappers and left them stranded. I reckon we'll never know who built it or why. But it's a solid cabin. Whoever built it knew what he was doing."

Ella said, "White Wolf told me his people have owned the valley for all time."

"The Cheyenne make that claim about the whole Great Plains," Chase Malone said.

"I can see their thinking," Ella said.

"Sure, I can, too," Chase Malone said. "But things are different now. The old days are gone. You can't turn time back like you can a clock. White Wolf knows that. He doesn't like it, but he knows it."

"I wonder if Reese Clarke knows it," Ella said.

"If he doesn't," Chase Malone said,

"he's sure going to find out."

The wagon ruts crossed the rail line. At the crossing I looked down the shining pair of rails that ran due east and west. They cut through the prairie as straight as two endless gunbarrels, straight west toward Sunbonnet, and finally on to California. Looking down the gleaming tracks to the point where they seemed to join, the thought flashed through my mind that I might see all the way to California if only my eyes were good enough. But the foolish idea passed as I recalled the maps I had studied in the library back home. The desert didn't go on forever — it only looked that way when you were out in it.

The buckboard jostled across the tracks. We came to a main road that ran alongside the rail line. Chase Malone turned the team west. Billy and Bobby, sensing something ahead, picked up the pace.

Then I saw something ahead, a blunt and top-heavy shape that stuck up from the horizon. As we came closer, I saw that it was a water tower for the steam engines. We passed it and crossed the bridge over the Sweetwater River. As Chase Malone had said, the river was shallow and wide down here. Out in the river bed I saw long, fish-shaped sandbars.

Sunbonnet was divided by the road and the railroad tracks. We drove past a grave-yard beside a stone church with a tall, pointed bell tower, frame houses with shaded porches and gingerbread decorations, and then into the business district. At the main intersection of Sunbonnet, across the street from the train depot, I saw a National Bank. It was built of stone like the church. On the other side of the street, at the end of a long row of false-fronted buildings, was a hotel and dining room called the Sunbonnet House.

Making our way through the heavy traffic of wagons and horses, we turned at the main intersection and headed toward the tracks. We made the turn and yielded to the water wagon that came up the street, spraying water. The water flowed in thin streams from a pipe at the rear of the wagon, making a smell of rain. The driver waved and called Chase Malone's name.

When we crossed the tracks, I noticed the water wagon had turned around instead of following the street to the saloon district. On the north side of the tracks the street was rutted and dusty.

The row of saloons and gambling houses were quiet in the late morning. There was no traffic. Few horses were tied at the tie rails. I saw some frame buildings that looked too big to be residences and too small to be hotels. The windows of these places were covered by dark curtains.

In front of a saloon called the Shoofly, a fat man swept the boardwalk. He glanced at us, then stopped his sweeping and looked again. "Malone? What the hell you doing in town?"

Chase Malone waved at the fat man, but he didn't answer. I looked back at him and saw that he was still watching us. Chase Malone drove the wagon almost all the way to the end of the street before he stopped the team in front of a big pink house. It was set back from the street and fenced like a mansion. The whole yard was enclosed by a pink slat fence.

"It seems strange to be back here," Ella said. Her voice was low and I thought she sounded sad.

"Coralee will be glad to see you," Chase Malone said, motioning for me to jump down.

I climbed off the wagon seat and helped Ella down. As she came down into my arms, her face leaned close to mine.

"Thank you, Boomer," she whispered.

I heard a door slam. I turned around at the sound of a deep, loud voice and saw that it belonged to a huge woman. "Ella!"

"Hello, Coralee," Ella said.

"You've come back!" Coralee looked down on us from the porch. She was built like a pyramid of flesh draped by black cloth. The shining black material of her dress flowed around her and down to her feet like a drape in a mortuary. Coralee took a few steps forward, but she didn't leave the porch.

"By God, it's good to see you, Ella! Take that bonnet and duster off. Let me see what that Malone has done to you." She threw a glance at Chase Malone like you might throw a rock at someone.

"Coralee," Chase Malone greeted her, touching the brim of his hat.

"He ain't done nothing to me," Ella said. "It feels strange to be back in town, that's all. I feel like crying and I don't know why."

"Why, you've been out in the desert too long, honey," Coralee said. "You look good though, considering you've been living like a goddam savage for the last year."

Chase Malone said, "Coralee, you don't have any idea how she's been living. You haven't left this palace for ten years." He waved his hand toward the pink house.

"Eight," Coralee said.

"If I told you Ella was living in a castle with twenty servants in the richest valley this side of paradise, you'd have to take my word for it."

"I wouldn't take your word on nothing, Malone. Besides, I know better. I read the newspaper. You're running some kind of outlaw camp up there on the Sweetwater, ain't you?"

Chase Malone said, "Don't believe everything you see in print, Coralee."

"It ain't true," Ella said.

Coralee looked down at Ella. "Well, you're back, anyway."

CHAPTER IX

The buckboard crossed the tracks and we headed toward the main intersection. I said that Coralee was the biggest woman I ever saw.

Chase Malone laughed. "A man wouldn't know what to do with one that big, would he?"

I said no before I figured out what he meant.

At the main intersection we turned east and made our way through the traffic to a livery. A sign over the doorway said *BLACKSMITH*, H. MacRae, Prop. After Billy and Bobby drank at a trough beside a corral, Chase Malone drove them into a vacant lot next door.

I followed Chase Malone back to the water trough. He took off his hat, slapped it on his leg, making dust fly. Then he worked the pump and sloshed water on his face, blindly reaching for his hip pocket. He brought out a blue bandanna and wiped his face. I felt the cool water when I rinsed my own face. I didn't have a bandanna, so I used my sleeves.

"By God," Chase Malone said, looking at me, "you do look like a gypsy. You haven't grown into my shirt yet. You're using a rope instead of a belt to hold up my pair of trousers." He laughed and clapped me on the shoulder. "We have to fix that. And I mean today."

Chase Malone pulled out a pocket watch and opened it. "Well, it's pushing noon," he said as he snapped it shut. "The first order of business is to scare up some chow."

As we walked in front of the open door beneath the *BLACKSMITH* sign, a man yelled from inside, "Howdy, Chase!"

Chase Malone backtracked and looked into the smoky gloom of the shop. "Why, howdy, Mac. How's business?"

"Been worse."

"I don't owe you any money, do I?"

"Hell, no."

Chase Malone laughed and waved at the man. We crossed the street and walked along the boardwalk with the noon crowd. We passed a hardware store that displayed a rifle in its window. Chase Malone took a long glance at the rifle and for a moment I thought he was going to stop, but then he went on. He did stop at a false-fronted building near the main intersection. He cupped his hands on the glass and looked in. I saw my own reflection in the glass. I wasn't sure what a gypsy looked like, but I saw that I looked strange — strange as a twelve-legged mule, as Boomer would have said back home.

The sign over the false-fronted building was painted in gold letters: SUNBONNET GLOBAL NEWS. On the glass window in smaller gold letters I read: COTTON TURNER, EDITOR-IN-CHIEF.

I followed Chase Malone to the dining room of the Sunbonnet House, off the main lobby of the hotel. The dining room was filled with the smell of food and the sounds of rattling dishes and voices of the diners. I stood behind and to one side of Chase Malone as he stood in the doorway, looking over the crowd. I couldn't see an empty table. Waitresses in white uniforms scurried from the kitchen to the tables like birds.

Then I saw a bearded man stand up and beckon to us. He waved a napkin. I walked behind Chase Malone as he made his way to the table by the window.

The bearded man held out his hand to shake. "Well, look who's in town," he said. "The notorious outlaw of the Sweetwater

Valley. And I see you brought one of your gun slicks with you."

Chase Malone laughed. "This gun slick is named Boomer Jones. Boomer, meet Cotton Turner. He's a newspaper editor who gets his news out at the town dump."

Cotton Turner shook my hand and our eyes met. His dark eyes appeared to glitter behind his eyeglasses. Though his sandy, full beard was streaked with gray, I knew he wasn't an old man. I guessed that he and Chase Malone were about the same age.

As we sat down, Cotton Turner said, "Now, is that any way to introduce a man?"

"I didn't say a thing about your manhood, Cotton."

Cotton Turner laughed and shook his head. "I see you still possess the sharpest tongue in the territory. I thought living out there in the desert with a woman might have a mellowing effect on you."

"Ella and I aren't under the same roof," Chase Malone said.

Cotton Turner started to say something when a redheaded waitress came to the table. Her starched uniform rustled like paper. Chase Malone asked the editor what he recommended.

The waitress giggled when Cotton Turner answered: "Special-of-the-Day. Throw yourself on the mercy of the chef."

"Two Specials," Chase Malone said. "And two coffees."

When the waitress had left, Cotton Turner said, "Chase, you should have been a newspaperman instead of a soldier or a squatter or farmer or whatever you are now. With your tongue and wit you could cut through the fog and smoke that often veils the truth."

Chase Malone said pleasantly, "If I were that kind of newspaperman, I never would have printed that letter from Reese Clarke."

White teeth showed through Cotton Turner's beard as he smiled. "I wondered if that epistle would have the effect of smoking you out of the desert."

Chase Malone nodded, but said nothing.

"I don't need to remind you — do I? — that a newspaper is obligated to serve as a forum for the citizens of the land. A newspaper must allow their voices to be heard as well as report news."

"A newspaper is obligated to report the truth," Chase Malone said.

"Ah," Cotton Turner sighed, "the truth is a many-faceted gem."

"The hell it is."

The editor raised a hand in protest. "I see the beginnings of an endless argument. But tell me —"

The redheaded waitress came with two plates of food balanced on one arm and two cups of coffee in her other hand. The Special-of-the-Day was stew. I dug in as soon as she set it in front of me. Before she carried away Cotton Turner's dishes she asked him if he wanted more mud. Solemnly, he said he did indeed She giggled again and refilled his coffee cup.

"Chase, tell me this," Cotton Turner asked, "do you doubt Reese Clark's sincerity?"

"Hell, yes," Chase Malone said around a mouthful of stew.

"Why?"

Chase Malone swallowed. "Reese Clarke has been trying to move me out of that valley for over a year. He's tried to scare me off and cuss me off my land. Now he's trying to turn public opinion against me — against me and Ella."

"I didn't think I'd live long enough to hear you worrying about public opinion." When Chase Malone went on eating and didn't answer, Cotton Turner spoke to me. "Why, I've seen Chase weaving down that street out there in full uniform, hunting for the sheriff. Oh, how he used to terrorize our poor sheriff. 'Hobbs,' he'd bellow, 'where are you? I'm hunting you, Hobbs!' " Cotton Turner laughed with the memory.

In my mind I pictured Chase Malone as a drunken soldier weaving down the main street of Sunbonnet.

Chase Malone took a swallow of coffee and said, "You might explain to the boy that Hobbs was the most worthless sheriff in the territory. If he heard a shot or if someone told him about a fight across the tracks, Hobbs would take off in the opposite direction hell for leather. I'd come looking for him just to get him to do the job he was paid to do. He didn't have any reason to be scared of me."

"Hobbs was reappointed last month," Cotton Turner said.

"No."

Cotton Turner nodded. "We lost our sheriff to the city of Cheyenne. He was a capable and fair-minded man. Even madams like Coralee liked him and co-operated with him. But when he asked for a raise, the city fathers, in their grand foresight, turned him down cold. They soon learned that he had had an offer from Cheyenne that paid half again the salary he made here. He left on the next train.

"As deputy, Hobbs fell back into the job. I wrote an editorial that suggested a good man must be paid a good salary, but it appears to have fallen on deaf ears. The city council and the mayor have convinced themselves that our former sheriff was greedy and we should be glad to be rid of him."

Chase Malone said, "This town's getting too big to have the village idiot serve as sheriff."

Cotton Turner motioned out the window. "Sunbonnet is one of the fastest-growing towns on the rail line. We're becoming a crossroads for north- and southbound freight traffic as well as being a main terminal for the railroad. There is even talk of building up that old army road that runs up in your direction. We're beginning to blossom now like Cheyenne did a few years back. The businessmen are filling their pockets, but not one is willing to return some of those profits to the city coffers. The sheriff's low salary is only one example. Our volunteer firemen need more than a few leaky buckets for fire-fighting equipment, but the businessmen won't hear of it. They have their fire barrels in the back alleys and that's good enough for them. Sunbonnet has never burned, Sunbonnet has never attracted hardcases or murderers, and the city council believes it never will." The editor turned his ink-stained hands palms up. "How can intelligent men be so stupid?"

Chase Malone washed down the last bite of stew with a swallow of coffee. "Hell, that's the story of civilization, Cotton."

"It would appear so."

"Why don't you sell off that newspaper, Cotton, and come up to the Sweetwater Valley? Stake your claim. I'll help you put up a cabin. Bring your books. Your biggest problem will be cutting enough wood in the summer so you stay lazy in the winter."

Cotton Turner smiled and shook his head. "No, that's not the life for me. And frankly, Chase, I don't think it's the life for you. If Reese Clarke wasn't bucking you, you'd probably get bored and come back here and run for mayor."

Chase Malone shrugged, but said nothing.

The editor went on, "Perhaps I take a certain pleasure in being a witness as well as a recorder of the demise of this newest experiment in civilization."

Chase Malone laughed. "You talk fancier than any man in the territory, Cotton.

You remind me of my departed father."
He drained his coffee cup and added,
"You come up to the valley for a visit this
summer. Bring your fishing pole. We'll
fish, drink, and argue. Can you top that?"

Cotton Turner's eyes narrowed behind
his eyeglasses as he glanced at me. I had
finished eating long ago and was restless.
"With this gunman and that outlaw hide-
away you're operating up there, I believe I
would fear for my safety."

Chase Malone said, "You sure are trying
to get me worked up to a frenzy, aren't
you? Well, editor-in-chief, listen to this:
What would you say if I told you that I
wrote a letter of my own to have printed in
your newspaper?"

"Does it pertain to some accusations
raised by one Reese Clarke?"

Chase Malone reached into his shirt
pocket and brought out a folded sheet of
paper. "Yep."

"Might it be classified as a rebuttal?"
"Yep."

"Then I'd say," Cotton Turner said,
taking the paper from Chase Malone's
hand, "that is one good way to sell newspapers."

Chase Malone swore as though disgusted, but he went on to tell Cotton

Turner about the work he and Ella had done on their quarter sections. The bearded editor asked a few questions and I got the idea he wanted to know more about Ella, but he seemed cautious in asking about her. From the way Chase Malone talked, you would have thought they were engaged to be married.

The three of us left the Sunbonnet House and walked down the boardwalk to the newspaper office. Cotton Turner shook hands with us and said the letter would be in the next issue of the *Global News*.

Chase Malone and I walked on to the hardware store that displayed the new Winchester in the window. This time Chase Malone stopped.

"By God," he said, "I'm getting an idea. Can you fire a rifle?"

"I don't know," I said. "I never tried."

"Well, you bring the wagon around to the back of this building," he said. "Pull it up snug to the loading dock, and then you come on inside."

I ran across the street and brought Billy and Bobby around to the alley behind the hardware store. I tied them at the dock and went inside through the back of the store. I walked up an aisle between a rack of single and double-edged axes and sledge ham-

150

mers, past a row of nail kegs, and found Chase Malone at the gun counter. A clean-shaven young clerk was pointing to the breech of a new Winchester that Chase Malone held in his hands.

"By God," Chase Malone said softly, as I walked up to him.

The clerk smiled confidently. "That weapon will do everything but walk and talk." He watched Chase Malone work the lever. "We take trade-ins. If you have another shoulder weapon, I believe I can give you the best price in town for it."

Chase Malone shook his head without taking his eyes from the Winchester. "All I own is an old Henry. I aim to keep it."

The clerk smiled as though he had seen everything once and nothing was new. "Henrys were fine weapons in their day. For long-range shooting they are as good as any shoulder weapon made — then or now. If yours has been well maintained, it may outlive all of us. Bring it in and I'll make you an estimate on what I can give you for it."

"I aim to keep the Henry," Chase Malone said again. "I'll buy this Winchester outright." He reached into his hip pocket and brought out a cash sack with a draw string. "And throw in four boxes of ammunition, too."

"You've made yourself a good buy, Mr. uh —"

Chase Malone handed him some bills and told him his name.

"Mr. Malone. Let's see, you have some change coming —" Something flickered in the clerk's eyes and the warm smile on his face twitched. "You said . . . you said your name was Chase Malone?"

"I did."

The clerk swallowed hard and stared. His shoes might have been nailed to the floor for all the moving he did.

"Hell, it's nothing to worry about, son," Chase Malone said. "I haven't bitten anyone as big as you for a whole month."

The clerk's mouth twitched into something that was almost a smile. He reached into a cash drawer and handed Chase Malone his change. Then he stepped back against the wall as though he expected to be shot.

"You got that list for my supplies, don't you?"

The clerk nodded once.

"Load the goods in the buckboard out back," Chase Malone said. "I'll come back and settle up with you in an hour or so."

Next door we went into the Wonder

Commercial Company, Dealers in Groceries, Wines & Liquors, Tobaccos, Cigars, and Pipes. At the counter Chase Malone handed another list to a clerk who wore garters on his sleeves and asked him to load those items in the buckboard tied at the loading dock behind the hardware store. The clerk read over the list, item by item.

I stood between the flour bins and a shelf of cheeses. Each flour bin bore a label: Pillsbury's Best, Defiance, Gold Medal, and Greeley Snowflake. On the opposite aisle were all kinds of cheeses: Swiss Cheese, Brickstein Cheese, Edam Cheese, Pineapple Cheese, and German Cheese.

Over the clerk's head I saw a sign that said, ORDERS ON THE LINE OF THE RAILROAD SOLICITED AND SATISFACTION GUARANTEED. I was struck by the passing thought that I could easily order something from the same suppliers that my father ordered from, and maybe I could even order something from his store.

"See anything you want, Boomer?" Chase Malone asked.

I shook my head.

We walked across the dampened street to *SKINNER CLOTHING*. Inside the door we were met by a dried-out lady. Her face looked pinched and I noticed that she eyed Chase Malone suspiciously. He carried the new rifle in one hand and four boxes of ammunition in the other. He traded stares with the lady before telling her to measure me for a complete outfit — three of everything.

She led me across the store to the displays of ready-made clothes. Without a word she quickly measured me for trousers and a shirt. Beneath the puffed short sleeves of her blouse, her sharp elbows jabbed the air. I picked out three sets of underwear, three pair of socks, and three light cotton shirts. I took one of each and stepped behind a curtain that the stern-faced lady held open for me.

When I came out, I felt as new as my new clothes. I saw Chase Malone grinning at me. He said my gypsy days were over.

The lady took the clothes I had been wearing along with my new ones and bundled them all in brown wrapping paper, tying the package with twine. Wordlessly, she accepted payment from Chase Malone. We started to leave, but before we got out the door, a strange sound came from the lady. I looked back and saw her mouth twisted open as though she was in pain.

"Have you taken to carrying a gun, Mr. Malone?" She almost spat out his name.

Chase Malone studied her and then said, "Your eyesight hasn't failed a bit, Mrs. Skinner."

She spoke through pursed lips. "We're peaceful folks here, Mr. Malone."

"So am I," Chase Malone said. He opened the door and started out, but then turned back. "Give my regards to Mr. Skinner. Tell him I'll buy him a drink if he can sneak out of the store this afternoon."

Mrs. Skinner's face colored and her cheeks puffed out until it seemed they might explode, but Chase Malone pulled the door shut and we stepped out into the hard sunlight of midday before anything happened.

"Can you top these city folks?" he asked.

We walked along the boardwalk to a small building whose sign said *BOOTS AND SADDLERY SHOP, HATS*. Inside, the shop smelled of leather. The owner, a small dark-skinned man that Chase Malone called Rodriguez, had many boots, belts, and saddles in the shop. Along the back wall I saw the hats.

Rodriguez spoke softly when he asked how he could serve Señor Malone. Chase Malone told him I needed a pair of boots and a hat — and a belt, he added with a laugh.

"And what kind of boots will you wear, *hijo?*"

The pair I liked were shiny with red and gold stitching running over the pointed toes in a swirl and up the sides. The heels were very high.

Chase Malone said, "A pair of plain working boots will go as fast as a pair of those fancy Texas boots, Boomer."

Rodriguez grinned and said that Señor Malone's words were true, but that I was blessed with the good eyes.

I found a pair of plain tan boots and belt that matched. The belt had a big square buckle that would keep anyone from slugging me in the stomach. The hat I ended up with was tan, too, with a plain, dark hatband.

The stiff cloth of my clothes rubbed against my skin in a tingling way as we walked along the boardwalk and crossed the street to the hardware store. I carried my lace-up shoes and the bundle of clothes, watching my boots with each step I took.

"Be careful you don't run into something," Chase Malone laughed. "I want to see the look on your face the first time you walk into a fresh cowpie."

I walked through the hardware store and waited in the wagon while Chase Malone paid the nervous clerk. The wagon bed was loaded with spools of barbed wire, posts, and boxes of staples. While we drove back through town to the saloon district, I noticed that quite a few men were moving in and out of the saloons and gambling houses. At the Shoofly several cowboys lounged in the shade by the batwing doors.

As we passed by, one of them yelled, "Malone!"

Chase Malone hauled back on the reins and stopped the team in the middle of the street. Among the men standing in the shade I recognized Buck Stone. His hat was shoved back on his head and his forehead looked as white as a hard-boiled egg.

"What the hell you doing in town?" Buck Stone shouted.

Chase Malone passed the reins to me and stood up, waving the new Winchester over his head. Buck Stone stepped out from the saloon to the edge of the board-walk and yanked out his revolver. He fired a shot in the air. All the way down the street cowboys and drifters tripped over their own boots as they dove for cover.

"Goddammit, Buck! My new rifle isn't

even loaded." Chase Malone stomped his foot down on the floorboards so hard the whole buckboard rocked. I pulled back on the reins to hold Billy and Bobby still.

Chase Malone jumped off the wagon. He tore open a box of ammunition and loaded the Winchester. "This thing loads as easy as pie."

Buck Stone fired again. I looked down the row of saloons and gambling houses and saw men poking their heads out of doorways and between buildings.

"Boomer, take the wagon down to Coralee's and fetch Ella," Chase Malone said. "She'll know where I am."

Even as I watched him, I didn't know whether to be scared or to laugh at him. Chase Malone had taken off his hat and thrown it into the wagon bed with the fencing and posts. His hair was as wild as ever and his eyes bulged out crazily. He was as excited as the first time I'd seen him when he came storming into Ella's yard.

"Go on, now!" he said to me.

I slapped the reins against Billy and Bobby's rumps and the buckboard lurched ahead. Then I heard four booming shots in close succession. They sounded much deeper than the shots from Buck Stone's revolver. I looked back and saw Chase

Malone standing in the middle of the rutted street, his feet spread wide, the new Winchester pointed in the air, and his mouth stretched into a wild grin.

"It works! This thing works as easy as pie!"

Buck Stone answered by firing another shot in the air. But when I looked back at Chase Malone, I pulled the walking team to a halt for I saw another man coming down the street. He was a short, square-built man with an odd, squat-legged way of walking. I saw a small star of reflected light high on the man's vest.

Buck Stone saw him first. He holstered his revolver and said, "Well, look here, boys."

Chase Malone turned to face him, still holding the rifle pointed in the air. The approaching man's step faltered, as though he only then recognized the man standing in the middle of the street.

"Hobbs, you worthless son-of-a-bitch," Chase Malone yelled, "you get on back to Sunday school where you belong."

I barely heard Sheriff Hobbs's voice: "What you doing here, Malone?"

"Me and Buck are shooting stars out of the sky," Chase Malone said. "And if you don't get back across the tracks, we'll shoot that one off your chest."

I was surprised to see Sheriff Hobbs walk backward faster than he had been walking forward. Buck Stone got to laughing so hard at the sight that he stumbled off the front of the boardwalk. He grabbed the hitchrack on his way down and swung around once like a thrown horseshoe.

Men began venturing out of doorways and from between buildings to watch. Some were grinning and murmuring. Sheriff Hobbs made the mistake of trying to turn around in the middle of a backward step. He tripped and went down. The audience of cowboys and drifters laughed aloud now and slapped one another.

As Sheriff Hobbs picked himself up, someone shouted, "Sober up, Shurf."

But amid the whooping and hollering I saw that Chase Malone wasn't laughing any more. He looked almost sad when he turned toward me. Our eyes met and then he gave me an impatient wave. I slapped the reins and headed down the street toward Coralee's pink house.

CHAPTER X

In the center of the pink door was a brass knocker in the shape of a bull's head. It was big, the size of a man's fist, and gleaming, pointed horns stuck out from it. I raised the head by the chin and let it fall. Coralee came to the door.

"I came for Ella," I said.

Coralee adjusted the sleeves of her shiny dress over her flabby arms. Then she looked down and saw me. "Boy, were you outside when all that shooting was going on a while ago?"

"It happened up the street," I said. "Chase Malone was only trying out his new rifle."

That was the wrong thing to say. Coralee's mouth fell open. "Right out there in the goddam street?"

I said, "Buck Stone started shooting first —"

"Buck Stone?" Coralee exclaimed. "Is he in town?"

I nodded, wishing I'd not said anything at all.

"I knew it." Coralee nodded her head as though she had found the answer to a big question. "When Malone comes to town, there's going to be some trouble. Trouble follows him like a goddam shadow. When Buck Stone hits town, it's the some song, second verse. That C Bar Ranch is the only spread I ever knew of that has a foreman who's twice as wild as any cowboy who works under him. Give that man a drink and you've got hell wearing spurs. But, Jesus, put him and Malone in town at the same time, and I wouldn't be surprised if the earth opened up and swallowed us all for punishment. And we would be damned lucky if that was all that happened to us."

Ella came to the door. She sounded tired when she said that we would have to be going if we aimed to get home by nightfall.

"Home!" Coralee snorted.

Ella went into a hallway and came back with her bonnet and duster. Everybody started saying goodbye to each other and take care, love, and so on. I could tell they were going to be there a while so I waited in the wagon.

When Ella came out we drove the team up to the Shoofly. On either side of the batwing doors were casement windows that showed a picture of an overflowing mug of beer. Beneath each mug was a curve of gold letters that read: *THE PRIDE OF SUNBONNET.*

The few cowboys and drifters who lounged in the shade in front of the Shoofly watched as I helped Ella down from the buckboard. When we stepped up on the boardwalk, a few of the men spoke to Ella and touched their hats.

One lanky cowboy had stopped whittling on a piece of wood and sat on his haunches with a jackknife poised in one hand and the carved wood in the other. Both knees were out of his denim trousers and one of his boots was held together with wire. When Ella stopped in front of him, he looked up and shoved his stained hat back on his head.

"Miz Ella," he said, greeting her.

"Why, howdy, Jake," Ella said.

I had never seen a man like Jake before. A mean scar ran up the side of his face, pulling one eye half shut. When he smiled up at Ella, I saw that all of his front teeth were gone.

"What are you doing in town?" Ella asked.

Jake looked away from her as though he didn't know what to say.

Ella asked, "Ain't you riding for the

White Ranch these days?"

"Nope."

"What happened?" Ella asked.

"Quit," Jake said. "Or got fired. I disremember."

Another man moved closer to us and scuffed a boot against the boardwalk. He was dressed like a cowboy, but somehow he didn't look like one. His skin was as pale as paper. Jake was as dark as an Indian.

The pale man said, "Jake got fired off the White Ranch, ma'am. I got fired off the Rocking JD. I cooked for that outfit for twelve years — up to a month ago. Lots of men got fired then."

"Why?" Ella asked.

"New owners."

"What does that have to do with it?" Ella asked. "Jake here is a top hand. Everybody knows that. Why, he could ramrod any ranch in the territory. And if you cooked for the same outfit for twelve years, you must not have poisoned anybody."

Jake laughed softly. He started whittling again, as though he had heard this conversation before. Curling slivers of wood fell to a pile below his spread knees.

"Overmanned," the cook said.

"What the hell does that mean?" Ella asked.

The cook grinned shyly. "I reckon it means there was too many cowboys for the cows. Anyhow, the new foreman fired a bunch."

"New foreman?"

"Yep."

Ella said, "The new owner must have cleaned house."

Jake spoke without looking up or stopping his whittling: "Owners, Miz Ella, owners."

"How many are there?" Ella asked in surprise.

"Several, what we heard," the cook said. "They're investors — a group of Easterners, what we heard. We don't know who they are. Anyhow, they picked up the White Ranch and combined it with the Rocking JD. The new foreman, he said they could run more cattle with fewer riders."

"I don't see the sense of that," Ella said. "Can they do it, Jake?"

Jake stopped whittling and looked up at her. He seemed to be squinting against the sun even though he was in the shade. "In good weather they can get away with it. But if they have to move stock in a hurry, they're shit out of luck."

"And Jake told the new ramrod just

that," the cook said fiercely. "I'm betting that's why he got fired. A lot of the other old hands got fired, too. The youngsters stayed on. They work hard, but they don't know a thing."

"What's the Rocking JD doing for cooks these days?" Ella asked. "Or are the new owners feeding the riders hay?"

The cook laughed bitterly. "They're using the JD as nothing more than an outcamp for the White Ranch. I reckon those boys are cooking for themselves, same as any line shack."

"Sounds like suicide to me," Ella said.

The cook smiled and dragged a hand across his cheek. I heard a scraping sound from his beard stubble.

"How long ago did all this happen?" Ella asked.

"We don't know when the sale of the White and JD was made," the cook said. "It was secret."

I got tired of standing in one place. I had been watching Jake whittle, but I decided he wasn't making anything in particular. I stepped up to the batwing doors and looked inside the saloon. The darkened, smoke-filled air looked gloomy. A few men stood in front of a wood bar that gleamed dully. Behind the bar I recognized the man who had been sweeping the boardwalk when we had first come to town. He stood in front of a long mirror that made a line of whiskey bottles look double. A few men sat at round tables playing cards. I looked for Chase Malone, but didn't see him.

Behind me I heard Ella ask, "Well, what're you boys planning?"

The cook said, "Most of the others already pulled out. Some went down into Colorado. Others rode for Montana. Me, I thought I'd stick it out here. I figured something would turn up. I got a fair reputation as a ranch cook. But now I don't know. I'm mighty low on money. Lately I've been thinking I'd better hunt for new pastures myself."

Ella asked, "How about you, Jake?"

Jake was slow in answering. I turned around to look at him. He had stopped whittling and was staring across the street. "I've punched cows and hunted strays in these parts for better'n twenty years. Many's the time I damn near died out there — been caught in storms, bit by rattlers, chased by Cheyenne bucks, one thing and another. A man hates to leave . . ."

Jake's voice trailed off and no one spoke for a long moment. A few other men had edged up close to hear what he was saying.

At last the cook said, "But you'll have to leave, Jake. You know you will."

Jake didn't say anything. But he didn't go back to his whittling, either.

"Buck Stone's in town," Ella said. "Have you boys talked to him about hiring on with the C Bar?"

Jake laughed softly. "Buck's talking about quitting hisself."

I glanced at Ella and saw a strange look cross her face. She started toward the batwing doors where I stood. "You boys come on inside and belly up to the bar. I'm buying."

Inside, the Shoofly smelled like whiskey, smoke, and sawdust. I looked down at my new boots and saw I was walking in saw-dust as I had in Chase Malone's saloon. Ella went to the polished bar and spoke to the bartender. I saw her hand him some money. Jake and the cook and a few other men who must have overheard Ella's offer stood nearby.

I noticed Buck Stone sitting at a table near the far wall, wearing his hat. Hanging on the wall over him was a stuffed buffalo head. I had never seen one before. I was surprised at how big it was. Pictures in library books didn't do them justice.

"Come on," Ella said as she walked past

me. I followed her to the table beneath the buffalo head. The buffalo's glass eyes were as brown as his coat.

I sat beside Ella, across from Buck Stone. She asked him where Chase Malone was. A half-gone bottle of whiskey and Chase Malone's new Winchester rifle were on the table.

Buck Stone didn't answer Ella. He looked at me. "Is this that same ragtag kid you told me about, or did you go out and hunt up a new one?"

"This is the same old one," Ella said. "Boomer's the hired hand." She looked around the saloon again. "Where's Chase?"

"He went back across the tracks," Buck said. "Claimed he had to see the printer."

Buck was getting ready to say something to me when Chase Malone came to the table and sat down. He explained that he had thought of some things that needed to be added to his letter that was going to be published in the newspaper. But before he could say anything else, Buck asked what a hired hand like me could do.

Chase Malone said, "You name it, he can do it. What Boomer can't do isn't worth doing."

I felt my face grow warm.

"Can he unwind a cyclone?" Buck Stone asked.

All of us laughed except Buck. From looking at him you'd have thought he was talking about a funeral. Ella told him I could do it if I put my mind to it. Buck nodded as though satisfied with that. Then I saw a smile slowly creep over his face. He reached for the small whiskey glass and almost knocked it over. I wondered how drunk he was.

Ella started in asking questions about why he was quitting the C Bar and what did he think he was doing and so on.

"Hold your horses, Ellie," Buck said. "I ain't quit the C Bar yet. How do these tales get around, anyhow? You listen to old Jake too much."

"You quitting or not?" Ella asked.

Buck said, "I believe I'm still working there."

Ella looked at Chase Malone. "Now, what the hell does that mean?"

"Buck was telling me that things are getting a little wild on the C Bar these days," Chase Malone said. "Reese Clarke has been wound tighter than a clock lately. He and Buck had a set-to last night. Buck came to town to cool off, that's all."

Ella asked, "What's the matter with Reese Clarke?"

"He probably isn't getting any," Chase Malone said.

"Maybe that's it," Buck said. "I hadn't thought of that."

"You have plenty of she-stuff on the C Bar, don't you?" Chase Malone asked.

"Only the four-legged kind," Buck said.

Ella shook her head at their talk. "Chase, did you hear about the White Ranch and the Rocking JD being sold to a bunch of Easterners?"

Chase Malone nodded.

"Well, what does it mean?"

Chase Malone shrugged. "It means we got a Texas-size ranch in the territory. I'm wondering if that's what has Reese Clarke wound up. Maybe he's afraid he's about to be swallowed. What do you think, Buck?"

"I don't know," Buck Stone said. "All I know is that I can't do a thing right around that spread any more. Reese Clarke's jumpier than a bug on a skillet. And I'm the one who gets jumped on."

Chase Malone said to Ella, "I told Buck he ought to draw his time and take a claim in the Sweetwater Valley. He'd make a good neighbor for us."

Buck closed one eye and looked at

Chase Malone. "You make it sound like you two are married up."

Chase Malone grinned and winked at me.

"Now, don't get started," Ella warned. "Here I am all mixed up about the way things are changing around here and all you two can think about is starting a brawl."

Chase Malone laid a hand on his new rifle. "Nobody's brawled with me since I bought this piece of iron."

"That's right," Buck said. "And that's the piece you'd better start sleeping with, too."

Chase Malone and Buck glanced at each other and in that instant I saw something pass between them, a respect between men that I saw and recognized even though I had never experienced it.

Ella put her hands up like she was pushing the two men apart. "That's enough. Come on. We got to be heading for home. We'll be late as it is."

She reached across the table and lifted Buck's Stetson up on his head so she could look into his eyes. "Buck, instead of staying around here paying rent on a bartender, why don't you come with us? I'll cook up a meal that you menfolk won't soon forget."

Slumped in the chair, Buck Stone looked up and asked, "Slow elk steaks, Ellie?"

Ella shoved his hat back down over his eyes. "The last steer we butchered wasn't wearing a C Bar, if that's what you mean."

CHAPTER XI

I rode with Buck Stone in the wagon bed. He stretched out on the fence posts and rested his head against a spool of barbed wire. His horse, Smoky, was tied on the back of the wagon. Buck had bought another bottle before leaving the saloon. Every time he uncorked it, he offered me a swig. I always shook my head. Once in a while he'd pass it up front to Chase Malone and Ella.

When we were out of sight of town and the water tower, we made the turn that took us across the tracks. The wagon jolted hard as the wheels bounced over the rails. Buck had been silent since leaving the saloon, but now he raised up on an elbow, scowling.

"By God," he said, "if you'd told me I'd ever be laying in the ass end of a buckboard with a roll of bob wire, a pair of land grabbing squatters, a slick-assed kid from nowhere, and a jug of bad whiskey in my hand, why, I'd have told you you was as crazy as a steer with his tail afire."

Chase Malone looked back and said, "If you don't like the ride back there, climb on that busted-down horse of yours."

"Be careful with that kind of talk," Buck said. "Smoky's my top cutting horse. There's nothing busted down about him."

"Get on him then," Chase Malone said over his shoulder.

"Naw, I'll be all right here," Buck mumbled. "Besides, Smoky won't let me ride him when I've been drinking."

"What?" Ella said in disbelief.

"That's right," Buck said. "If Smoky smells whiskey on me, he won't let me on."

Ella laughed. "I've never heard of such a thing."

"You haven't?" Buck asked. He winked at me. "My grandma was the same way. Damn near drove my granddaddy crazy."

Chase Malone laughed. Ella reached back, pulled Buck's hat off his head and swatted him with it. Chase Malone got to laughing so hard that he almost lost the reins. He doubled over and stomped his boots on the floorboards.

As we followed the old army road through the open desert that afternoon, Buck drank most of his whiskey, talked off and on about how he wished he was a boy like me, and sang songs. The songs mostly sounded alike and had words about cattle, going home, and lost love. Then Buck sank into a drunken silence and finally slept, open-mouthed and reeking of liquor.

I watched Buck Stone while he slept. His clothes were worn without being worn out. The hat that slanted across his face was darkened with age and use. Sweat stains crept up around the rattlesnake hatband. The brim was bent and discolored on the right side where he had grabbed it to take it off or to pull it down against the sun. The plain brown walnut grips on the handle of his Colt's revolver stuck out of a hard leather holster on his right hip. I couldn't understand why Buck Stone wanted to be a boy like me when I wanted to be a man like him.

"Ain't we there yet?" Buck asked. After nearly two hours' sleep he had awakened with a series of moans and snorts. "Hell," he said, looking around, "we ain't nowhere. This is the slow boat. I'm hungry as a bear after winter."

"Another hour or so," Ella said.

Buck lay back, made a smoke, and studied me. "I ain't got you figured, slick. All I know is what I hear about you. From what I hear, nobody knows who you are or where you're from."

Ella turned in the wagon seat. "It's nobody's business either."

"Let him fight his own battles, Ellie," Buck said. "I'm just asking. There's no harm in asking. Are you on the dodge, slick?"

"Mind your manners, Buck," Ella said.

"You're sweet on him, ain't you?"

"You bet," Ella said. I felt the warmth of her hand as it rested on my shoulder.

"A man's past is his own business," Buck said. "Ellie's right about that. I've got riders on the C Bar that nobody knows their right names. They pick up a nickname and use it for a handle. Why, I've had good working men draw their time and ride out just because they heard an out-of-town lawman was staying at the Sunbonnet House."

Buck raised up on an elbow, hawked, and spat over the side of the wagon. "Tasted like cheap whiskey," he mumbled. He laid back down, smoked some more, and then said to me, "What do you figure on doing with yourself, slick?"

I suddenly felt too embarrassed to answer.

"You aim to hire on as a cowboy?" he asked.

I nodded, but I couldn't match his stare. "Don't do it."

Ella said, "Buck . . ."

"No, I mean it," he said. "A cowpuncher works harder than anybody and ends up with nothing. I've rode behind steers since I was old enough to saddle my own horse. What do I have now? Two horses, a saddle, and a change of clothes. I know what I'm talking about when I say they ain't nobody who works harder than a goddam cowboy. Nobody. You're up before the sun, and you're lucky to be in the sack before midnight — every day, seven days a week. And what do you get for it? I'll tell you. You get the honor of making some cattleman rich, that's what. And when you get too old to work, it's goodbye, cowboy. An old cowhand is as worthless as tits on a steer. Why, look at old Jake. He's all busted up from working his ass off and from living in the saddle for forty years. He's through. And he's the only one who hasn't figured it out yet."

"If it's as bad as you say, Buck," Ella asked, "why do you stay with it?"

Buck Stone looked back at his trailing horse, mashing out the live stub of his cigarette in his bare fingers. "A man learns his ways. He don't change."

"Why not?" Ella asked. "Look at Chase. He's homesteading. Before that he was a soldier. There's no telling what he did before that. Some say he was a lawyer. Is that true, Chase?"

I saw Chase Malone barely raise his shoulders in a shrug.

Ella said, "A man can change his ways if he wants to."

"Ellie," Buck Stone said, "you wear me out with talk. Every time I say something, you pick it apart and throw a passel of questions at me. You ought to get together with Encyclopedia Charlie."

Without thinking I asked, "Who's he?"

"Aw," Buck said, "he's just another meathead cowboy. He memorized a book called *Ten Thousand Things Worth Knowing*. Now he thinks he knows everything. He was a fair cowboy before that."

"He memorized a whole book?" I asked.

Buck Stone nodded sourly.

"How?"

"Wintering by hisself in the north camp. He had to do something to keep from going crazy, I reckon. Year before we had two men up there, but they got cabin fever so bad they damn near killed each other. They still ain't on speaking terms.

"Hell, I used to like Charlie before he

learned that book. Now, every time I see him coming, I got to think up something to do so I can get away. You can't say anything to him without him going into some long palaver. I can't even say, 'Well, it sure looks like rain,' without old Encyclopedia Charlie telling me all about cloud formations and such. He even has a long talk he gives about why we can see rainbows. Who gives a damn? Not me. I just look at them and ride on. Same with rain. I don't care about the clouds. I can usually feel a rain coming. Sometimes I'm right, sometimes I'm wrong. I put on my slicker and that's the end of it." He fell silent as he looked out across the prairie. Then he said, "But what I was getting to was that Ellie ought to get hooked up with Encyclopedia Charlie. She could ask the questions and he could spout off with the answers."

Ella said, "Go back to sleep, Buck."

"I can't," Buck said. "You got me wokened up now. When do we eat?"

I got tired of sitting in one place. I'd been using my bundle of clothes as a cushion against the jolting wagon. But I felt my legs cramping. I stood up and faced the front of the buckboard. To keep my balance, I put my hands on Ella's shoulders. She smiled up at me.

I saw the red rocks ahead, sticking out of the earth like sores. From that distance there was no way of knowing that the rocks were the beginnings of the cliffs that bordered the Sweetwater Valley.

It was dusk when we followed the wagon ruts through the break in the rocks, dropped down a slope, and crossed the river. Billy and Bobby wanted to stop in midstream to drink and cool their hoofs, but Chase Malone urged them on, telling them we were almost home. I thought of my pony and again felt a twinge of fear that he would be gone. I couldn't push the thought away as we started up the darkening valley. I breathed in the sweet, moist air that smelled of water and grass and looked ahead.

It was nearly dark by the time we reached the cabin. But I saw my pony inside the corral. He whinnied at us. Chase Malone and I unloaded the buckboard and took care of the team while Ella started supper. Buck had unsaddled his horse, watered and fed him and was wiping him down when I turned the team in the corral with the other horses. Chase Malone had gone into the cabin. I held a lantern near Buck and asked if he wanted to put Smoky in the corral.

"I did," he said, "until I seen Malone's in there."

"Don't you like that big horse?" I asked.

"It ain't that," Buck said. "Malone's horse don't like anybody — or anything. He ain't good for anything. Say, who's that little pony belong to? Injun pony, ain't he?"

"He's mine," I said.

"Yeah? Where'd you get him?"

"An Indian chief gave him to me."

"Is that a fact," Buck said. His tone of voice made me wonder if he thought I was making it up. "And what was this chief's name?"

"White Wolf."

"White Wolf?" Buck said. "Well, I'll be damned. And you say he gave him to you? I'll be damned. I never heard of White Wolf giving anything away. He must have taken a shine to you, slick."

As Ella had promised, we had a big supper of steaks, potatoes, peas and carrots, and hot cornbread with honey. For dessert she brought a cherry pie out of the oven. It was a late supper and I couldn't remember ever feeling so hungry. After putting away two helpings of everything, I'd thought I was full, but then the cherry pie came out. I found room for two pieces.

Buck Stone called them slabs. He leaned back in his chair, sipped coffee, and wondered aloud how any boy as skinny as me could eat so many slabs of pie.

"Some of it is probably going into those new boots," Chase Malone said.

Buck Stone and I cleaned up the supper dishes that night. I dried while Ella sat with Chase Malone at the table. Buck mentioned seeing my pony in the corral. That got Ella started on the story of her dream and how she had disguised my whiteheaded Indian pony.

Buck Stone, his sleeves rolled high up on his white arms, scrubbed dishes and pans while Ella talked. He kept saying "I'll be damned, Ellie, I'll be damned." He had just finished saying it and handing the black skillet to me when I heard the riders coming. The sounds of hoofs pounding the earth grew louder like drums in a march. I knew they were coming into the yard.

"Buck! Buck Stone! You in there?"

Buck picked up a lantern and opened the cabin door. He held the lantern high. I moved behind him and saw four riders sitting their horses in the yard.

"Bob?" Buck asked. "Is that you?"

"Yeah."

"Well, step down," Buck said. "Have

some coffee. Who's that with you? Hank?"

"Yep," one of the men answered. "Smiley and young Texas is with us."

Bob said, "We went to town, hunting you. We heard you'd rode off with Malone."

None of the cowboys dismounted. Buck stepped outside and was looking up at them when Chase Malone walked past me and went outside, too.

"Well, you found me," Buck said. "What's so goddam important?"

No one answered for a long moment. Then Bob said, "Mr. Clarke sent us. He said for us to bring you back."

"He sent all four of you?" Buck snorted. He turned to Chase Malone. "Next time you get ornery with me, remember that it takes four grown men to rope me and carry me home."

The four riders laughed nervously.

Buck Stone looked back at them and said, "Well, I ain't ready."

Hank asked, "When are you going to be ready?"

The other three laughed.

"How should I know?" Buck said. "You just go tell Reese Clarke I'll be back before sunup."

"Naw," Bob said slowly. "Mr. Clarke, he

said we shouldn't come back without you."

Buck said, "So I have to take you men home. Is that it? Ain't this something? You ever see a thing like this, Chase?"

Chase Malone said he hadn't. "Are you boys in any hurry to get back to the C Bar?"

None of them answered until the lean cowboy named Hank punched his hat back on his head. "Hell, no, we ain't in no hurry. I wasn't in no hurry to leave Sunbonnet. Bob was."

Bob said, "We had a job to do."

The third cowboy, an older man, said, "I didn't want this job at all."

"Me, neither," Hank said.

"Then why did you take it?" Buck asked with a laugh.

"You know why," Hank answered. "It was either that or quit. I'm too far in debt to the C Bar to quit."

"Me, too," Bob admitted.

"Ain't you a pitiful bunch," Buck said.

"We don't make as much money as you do," Bob said.

"Well, then why don't you take my job over?" Buck said. "I'll give it to you."

"In town we heard you was quitting," the older rider said. "That true?"

"Nope," Buck said. "Not today, any-how."

"How about tomorrow?" Hank asked.

"Tomorrow's a brand-new day," Buck answered. "Say, my neck's getting sore from looking up at you boys and I'm tired of holding this here lantern. Now, you either step down off them C Bar plugs or ride off, hear?"

Bob looked at the other three riders, then said to Buck, "We ain't supposed to be here at all. You ain't, either. Those was the orders."

"Well, why don't you boys go follow them orders," Buck Stone said. "I ain't going to bother with them."

None of the four riders moved. I felt Ella standing close behind me. Though no one seemed angry, there was a tenseness in the air as though everyone expected something to happen, but no one knew what.

The tense silence was finally broken by Chase Malone: "Buck and me were fixing to ride up to my place. Why don't you boys come up and have a drink with us?"

The silence fell again like a curtain. The four riders sat their horses, looking at the ground between them and Buck and Chase Malone. The yellow light of the lantern didn't carry far and the cowboys were surrounded by darkness. On the edge of this darkness sat the fourth rider. I couldn't see him well, but I noticed that he dressed fancier than the others and he looked quite a bit younger.

At last the tall cowboy named Hank said, "By God, I could use a drink."

That broke it. The men relaxed and looked at one another, nodding their heads. Chase Malone and Buck got their hats and went out to the corral. When they had their horses saddled, they rode back to the cabin where Ella and I stood. Buck handed the lantern down to her.

"Come on up, Ellie," Buck said.

Ella shook her head. "It's been too long a day for me. You go on."

Buck turned his horse and Chase Malone started to follow, but then reined up. He looked down at me and said, "You coming, Boomer?"

I looked at Ella. She smiled and said, "You might as well go on with the rest of the men. Just don't forget to come home."

Chase Malone kicked his foot out of the stirrup and reached down for me. I put my new boot in the stirrup and grasped his hand. He pulled me up behind him.

Buck said I was crazy to ride double on that animal, and then spurred his own horse as he waved goodbye to Ella. I didn't know whether Chase Malone kicked his big horse or whether he took off just to keep up with Buck Stone, but I didn't even have a chance to suck in a breath when the animal leaped away as though shot.

The wind tore at my bare head as I realized I'd forgotten my new hat. My eyes watered when I looked into the darkness that we plunged into, and I heard the four riders pounding up the road behind us. One had pulled up close as though he wanted to overtake us. I heard somebody whooping. I looked back and could barely make out the shapes of riders crashing through the night at a dead run.

By the time we reached the looming shape of the saloon all the riders were whooping and hollering. Six horses pulled up in a flurry of dust that I smelled more than saw. I jumped off the big horse. Over the sounds of heaving animals and men I heard someone tell Buck he was a crazy bastard.

"It takes more than one crazy bastard to make a horse race," Buck said.

Chase Malone lighted lanterns inside his saloon. The men came in, still breathing hard, pounding feet, and jangling spurs. They pulled up chairs around a table in the center of the saloon. I brought a ladderback chair and sat beside Buck. He sat backward on a broken chair. Chase Malone carried a bottle and seven tin cups to the table. He poured and then pulled a chair up himself.

The men drank in silence and Chase Malone poured another round. I was still working on the first round. No one said much until the second round was half gone.

"Worst whiskey I ever swallered," Buck said.

Chase Malone smiled.

Hank said, "It gets better as you go."

"Shore does," the older cowboy said. I'd heard someone call him Smiley. It seemed like a funny name to me because he was sad-faced.

I guessed the young Texan was only eighteen or nineteen. He wore a bright scarf around his neck and silver conchos around his hatband. He had a cocky way about him. He made a point of not looking at me.

Hank said, "This place sure beats that old army tent you was living in when you first moved into the valley. That thing was hotter than fire in the summer, wasn't it?"

Chase Malone nodded. "If a man died in

one, he'd never know the difference."

While the men chuckled, the Texan laughed aloud, his voice booming through the saloon. The men fell into silence until Hank told a joke about a preacher's daughter who fell into a well. When he finished he said, "Smiley, tell the boys here about that argument you heard between Windy Will and that horse of his. What's that club-footed critter named?"

"Cyclone," Smiley said.

"Yeah, Cyclone," Hank laughed. "Tell the boys about it."

Smiley said, "I happened to be coming around the barn the other day when I heard Windy Will shouting and yelling, having a terrible bad argument with someone. It sounded so hot that I stopped beside the barn where he couldn't see me. I didn't want any part of it. Oh, you should have heard it. Windy was giving somebody a whole load of hell. Only the odd thing was, I couldn't hear anybody arguing back. My curiosity got me, so I peeked around the corner of the barn. There was Windy Will, standing nose to nose with his horse, Cyclone. 'Why, you no good son-of-a-bitch,' Windy says, 'how do you expect me to believe a stupid thing like that? You must think I'm as crazy as you are if you think I'm going to swallow something as wild as that.' Then Windy seen me watching. He got a funny look on his face and backed off a couple of steps. So I says, 'What ain't true, Windy?' And old Windy points to Cyclone and says, 'Aw, ask him.' "

The men laughed long and hard at that.

"By god, I've heard enough of this," Bob said. "Malone, what the hell did you put in this whiskey?"

"Same as always," Chase Malone said. "Four plugs of tobacco, a box of rat poison, a dash of salt."

Hank said, "I believe you overdid the salt on this batch, Malone."

"I'll be more careful next time."

"You do that."

Smiley said, "Chase, I hope you got a new deck of cards by now."

"That old deck is just getting broken in," Chase Malone said.

"Broken in, hell," Smiley said. "They damn near got the numbers wore off them. And the queen of spades and ace of diamonds got the corners busted off."

"Yeah, Malone," Hank said, "last month — or was it two months ago? I disremember — me and Shorty had a fighting argument over one of them cards. We couldn't read the numbers. He swore it was the ace of hearts. But I knowed it was the deuce."

"How did you know that?" Chase Malone asked.

"I ain't saying."

"Well, how did you settle the argument?"

"Aw, we finally throwed the card out. It was either that or kill each other."

As the late hour and the few sips of whiskey caught up with me, the men's voices began to run together until they became one even sound like a river, marked by the young Texan's occasional laughter. I heard the men talking about spring roundup, branding, and the sale of the White Ranch and the Rocking JD. From far away I heard someone talk about the buildings of the White Ranch being painted white. I knew I'd seen such a place, but I drifted off to sleep without remembering where. The next thing I knew Chase Malone was shaking me. I was surprised to look around an empty saloon.

"You'd better run back to Ella's," he said. "You could stay here tonight, but Ella's expecting you. If you don't show, she'll come looking for you."

I stood up and shook the haze of sleep out of my head. Chase Malone followed me to the porch of the saloon. I didn't know what time it was, but it felt late, close to midnight, I guessed.

"Be sure to tap on Ella's door and let her know you're there," he said. "Tell her I'll be down for breakfast in the morning. We'll start on that south fence tomorrow."

The moon was high up over the cliffs. It cast white light into the Sweetwater Valley, making a tangle of shadows in the trees and in the brush along the river. I remembered something Ella had said about Reese Clarke acting like he was moonstruck, and I wondered how long I would have to be in the moonlight before the madness hit me. I walked as fast as I could without stumbling down the wagon ruts toward Ella's cabin, wishing I'd ridden the roan pony. When you own a good horse, walking feels like a sin.

A dim light burned inside the cabin. The curtained window beside the door glowed like a single eye. Ella answered my knock and handed me a lantern that was turned low. I told her Chase Malone planned to have breakfast with us and we were going to start work on the fence in the morning. Ella's face was puffy from sleep and her loose hair was bunched around her face. She nodded sleepily and said good night.

When I went into the barn all I could think about was climbing under the blankets and going to sleep. I undressed and blew out the lamp. But when I stretched out in the bunk and began to relax, a strange feeling came over me. I sat up suddenly, listening hard.

I wanted to call out, Who's there? but I couldn't. In the strained silence I heard nothing but my own heartbeat. I got out of bed and pulled on my boots. I was trying to decide whether I should light the lantern when I heard the back door squeak on its hinge. Then I saw someone move across a patch of white moonlight down there.

I ran through the runway of the barn and leaped through the doorway that opened into the corral. No one was there except the horses. Though I'd only had a glimpse of a figure moving through the doorway, I'd recognized her. It was the Indian girl from White Wolf's camp.

CHAPTER XII

After breakfast I helped Chase Malone hook up Billy and Bobby to the buckboard. Ella waved goodbye to us when we drove out of the yard and headed down the valley toward the south boundary of Ella's claim. I looked back and saw my pony standing with his head over the top pole of the corral, watching us leave. Before breakfast I had fed the horses and combed out the pony. The make-up still covered the white on his head and showed no signs of wearing off. Dust stuck to it and when I had tried to brush it off the pony's jaw, I'd got red make-up on my fingers.

I said, "The pony wants to come with us."

Chase Malone glanced back and said, "He's used to being with Billy and Bobby, I reckon. What are you going to name that Indian cayuse?"

"I don't know," I said. I hadn't been able to think of a good name.

"How about Cyclone?" Chase Malone asked. "Then you could argue with him."

On the way down the valley I saw a haze of smoke coming out of the trees where White Wolf was camped. I hadn't told Chase Malone or Ella about seeing the Indian girl last night. I thought the story would sound pretty wild. I couldn't think of any good reason for her to be in that barn in the middle of the night.

"Well, I see old White Wolf is still in the valley," Chase Malone said.

I looked into the trees below the drifting smoke, but I couldn't see anything. Chase Malone drove the wagon on south until we reached a pile of rocks beside the wagon ruts. He turned east and stopped the wagon at another stack of rocks near the tree line.

"The first job," he said, looking back into the cottonwoods and tangle of willows, "is to snake a wire all the way back to the riverbank. Sometimes during a change of weather, the cattle will get back in there and mill around and drift southward. So we'll put a fence in to stop them. One good thing — we don't have to worry about keeping a straight line. Ella doesn't have any neighbors yet."

I looked out across the grassland toward the south end of the valley and tried to imagine other people living there. "Do you think she ever will?"

Chase Malone climbed off the wagon seat, reached into the back of the buckboard, and tipped up a spool of barbed wire. "That may depend on whether we can stick it out here. Plenty of folks would like to settle here in the Sweetwater country, but they're afraid. Cattlemen have had the run of this valley for thirty years."

"But no one owns the valley?" I asked. "Not even Reese Clarke?"

"Nope, not even Reese Clarke," Chase Malone said. "But you can bet he lies awake at night, wishing he owned this valley. He probably has nightmares about homesteaders flocking in here like birds to corn."

"Will they?"

"It's likely," Chase Malone said, pulling heavy gloves on his hands. "But there's no telling when. Like I told you once, you'll live to see this whole territory settled up if you stay around these parts. That's in the cards no matter what Reese Clarke thinks he can do about it. You can't stop progress. All you can do is ride with it."

I steadied the spool while Chase Malone looped the end of the barbed wire around his gloved hand and worked his way back into the trees. I soon lost sight of him.

When the spool stopped turning, he yelled
for me to bring the hammer and a handful
of staples. I opened the blue box and
brought out as many as I could hold,
feeling some sharp points dig into my
hand. On all four sides of the blue staple
box was a motto that read like a poem:

> One staple
> Is twice as good as
> One nail.

I followed the barbed wire through the
trees and brush and found Chase Malone
at the riverbank. He had wrapped the wire
around a thick cottonwood tree that leaned
out over the water. He held the wire snug
while I drove in several staples. Then we
worked our way back to the buckboard.
Chase Malone pulled the wire tight as we
went, and I stapled it to tree trunks along
the way. The first strand was almost as
high as my chest. We strung out another,
knee high, then a third between the two.

"That takes care of the easy part," Chase
Malone said when we came out of the trees
the third time. "From now on we have to
put in posts."

He pointed across the valley to the red
cliffs. "Take a straight line and run it from

here due west all the way to the cliffs, Boomer. That's how our fence has to go."

"That's a lot of fence," I said doubtfully.

"We can do it."

Chase Malone took the pick from the wagon bed, stepped off several paces from the tree line, and started digging. The point of the pick came down from high over his head and stabbed into the spikes of green grass. The sod was suddenly opened, baring the rich soil beneath. He dug down two feet before hitting rock.

Chase Malone backed away and told me to clean out the loose soil with the spade. When I had the dirt cleared away, he went to work on the rocks. They were all rounded and ranged in size from a man's fist to a large melon. Each rock had to be loosened and lifted out of the hole.

When the hole was about three feet deep, Chase Malone brought a fence post from the wagon. He held it upright in the hole while I stacked rocks around it. Then he shoveled the moist soil back into the hole, packing it as he went.

"Well, there's the first one," Chase Malone said, looking at me with approval. "The work goes fast with the two of us. I put in the north fence by myself. It took me all morning just to get a couple of posts in."

We were digging the hole for the third post when I happened to look up the valley and saw White Wolf. He stood close to the tree line, near his camp, watching us. I waved, but he didn't wave back. He stood alone, still and watchful.

Chase Malone didn't see White Wolf until I told him. He lifted a stone from the bottom of the post hole and set it on the ground at my feet. He wiped his brow and looked up the valley.

I said, "He just stands there and watches."

"How long?"

"I first saw him about ten minutes ago. I don't know how long he had been there."

"Well, he's probably curious about what we're doing."

"He doesn't act friendly," I said. "I waved at him, but he wouldn't wave back."

"You won't find a Cheyenne who likes fences," Chase Malone said, as he pulled the third fence post out of the wagon bed. "He's probably not too happy about us stringing a wire across the valley. He'll get used to the idea in time."

By noon we were digging the sixth post hole. We would have been farther along, but we ran into a boulder in the fifth hole and we dug around it for quite a while before deciding that it was too big to move. We had to fill the hole and start again a few feet ahead.

White Wolf was gone when we drove the wagon back up the valley toward the cabin. The sun shone high in the sky over the Sweetwater Valley, making the air almost hot. A slight breeze from the motion of the wagon cooled my sweat.

Ella had lunch waiting for us. When Chase Malone told her how much work we'd done, Ella said that I was really earning my wages.

I said, "I've never said my thank-yous for buying my new clothes. I can't take any wages until I've worked off all the expense I've caused you."

Ella looked at me carefully and smiled in a way that embarrassed me.

Chase Malone said, "I admire your attitude, Boomer. But as long as you're working for us, you'll have spending money. A man's got to have a little change in his pocket."

On the way back to the south boundary after lunch we saw a long cloud of dust rising along the base of the red cliffs. I thought a rider was coming.

Chase Malone pulled the team to a halt and we sat watching a low shape coming out of the dust at a full run. It cut an angle toward us and streaked across the field of grass. I heard a strange rumbling sound, like drums far away.

Chase Malone laughed. "I wish I'd brought my new rifle."

"Who is it?"

"Old One Eye," he said. "That locoed steer. All he does is run. Crazy as hell."

As he came closer I saw the red steer. He wasn't raising much dust now as he galloped across the high grass. He was fifty or sixty yards away when he veered off suddenly and cut northward at a dead run. Billy and Bobby had been getting nervous, pawing the ground and bobbing their heads, but they calmed when the steer turned and found a new course for his madness.

Chase Malone slapped the reins and said, "By God, that's going to be your next job, Boomer."

"What?"

"Killing that outlaw steer," he said. "I almost forgot about him. Now that we're putting in the south fence, we can't let him run. He'll be tearing it out twice a week."

"How am I going to kill him?" I asked.

Chase Malone laughed. "Why, you're going to climb on that little Indian pony of yours and run the one-eyed bastard down. Then you're going to put a bullet through his good eye."

"I don't know how to shoot a gun," I said.

"I know that," Chase Malone said. "But you're going to learn — starting this evening."

As we passed by the smoke rising from White Wolf's camp, I saw something moving in the trees. It was the girl. She stepped out to the edge of the tree line as we passed by. Chase Malone waved and called something to her in Cheyenne, but she didn't wave back. She stood and watched us the way White Wolf had earlier in the day.

"Birdy sure isn't speaking to me today," Chase Malone said.

I said, "When I went to White Wolf's camp, she jumped me from behind and tried to stab me with a knife."

"She did?" Chase Malone asked in surprise.

I nodded. "She would have, too, if White Wolf hadn't pulled her off me. Then last night I saw her running out of the barn when I came back from your place."

Chase Malone looked at me thoughtfully as the wagon rolled along the wagon ruts. "Was she carrying her knife?"

"Don't you believe me?" I suddenly wished I'd kept my mouth shut.

"Hell, yes, I believe you, Boomer. But what do you think she was doing in the barn that late at night?"

"I don't know," I said. "I thought she might be trying to steal my pony."

He laughed. "Well, I'll tell you one thing. If she was aiming to cut you open last night, she would have done it. And if she wanted that pony, she'd have taken him."

Chase Malone turned the wagon at the pile of rocks and drove the team toward the new fence line. "I could take a wild guess and say that she was in the barn for another reason."

"What?" I asked.

He stepped the wagon near the last fence post we had put in. "I'd say she's in love with you, boy."

Chase Malone laughed as he jumped off the wagon seat. When he looked up at me I could see he was enjoying himself. "What's the matter, Boomer?" he asked, laughing.

I couldn't think of anything to say that would shut him up.

"Doesn't that lightheaded Cheyenne gal

appeal to you?" he asked. "You got yourself an Indian horse. Now all you need is
an Indian gal."

"You're the one who's lightheaded," I
said, but it only made him laugh harder.

As we worked that afternoon I saw
someone moving in the trees near the
fence line. I was pretty sure it was the girl,
but I made a point of not looking too hard.
I was glad Chase Malone was too busy
working to see her — or to rawhide me. By
late afternoon we had fourteen posts in.

We sighted down the row of posts and
admired them for being so well lined up.

"They're as straight as a squad of soldiers," he said. Then he added, "And
they're about as smart, too."

"By God, this work is going fast," he said
as we drove back up the valley. "We'll have
the fence done in a week or ten days. It
took me a month to get the north fence in.
I was sober, too."

We ate supper before sundown that evening. When Ella asked how the fence was
going, Chase Malone swore and put on an
act about not being able to get any work
out of me. Ella went along with it and
asked him why.

"The hired man's in love," Chase
Malone said. "He was mooning around

worse than a cow in heat. He's so bad in love I believe he's about to melt."

Ella cocked her hips and smoothed her hair. "Who's the hired man in love with?"

"That little gal in White Wolf's camp," Chase Malone said. "He thinks she's a straight line to heaven."

"Oh," Ella said, as though disappointed. "I was hoping he was in love with me."

They looked at me, waiting for me to say something.

"I am, Ella," I said, "real bad."

They laughed. Chase Malone said he admired a boy who could take a ribbing. Then, over a dessert of cherry pie, he told Ella what the Indian girl had done to me in White Wolf's camp and that I had seen her in the barn last night.

"So that's why she was so mad at you when I came and got you out of White Wolf's tepee," Ella said. "I wondered what had been going on between you two. I thought she hated you because you were so handsome. But I reckon Chase is right. She hates you because she's in love with you."

When we finished dessert, Chase Malone stood up and said he and I had to get moving if we aimed to get any shooting in before dark.

Ella asked, "Are you going to teach Boomer how to shoot that new Winchester?"

Chase Malone shook his head. "The new one shoots by itself. I'm going to show him how to fire the Henry."

"That old rifle of yours?" Ella asked.

He nodded. "That old Henry is powerful enough to shoot through a mountain. And it's a repeater. You load it on Sunday and fire it all week."

"Will Boomer need a rifle that powerful?" Ella asked.

"Damn right, he will," Chase Malone said. "Boomer's going after One Eye."

"What?" Ella exclaimed.

Chase Malone nodded. "Now that we're getting the south fence, we can't let that locoed steer run any more. Hell tear out fence as fast as we put it up. You've seen that north fence after he's been through it, haven't you? Besides, he keeps all the other stock worked up. It's time for somebody to run him down and beef him."

Ella asked, "Why don't you do it yourself?"

"It's too dangerous," Chase Malone said. "Why should I risk my butt when I've got a hired man who's getting paid to risk his?"

Ella shook her head at Chase Malone. I

followed him out of the cabin to the corral. We saddled our horses and rode up to the saloon. My pony was skitterish at first, but by the time we reached the saloon he had settled down. Chase Malone went inside to get the two rifles while I waited out front, holding the reins of his big horse.

When Chase Malone came out, he carried two rifles and a burlap sack that rattled with the noise of empty tin cans. He handed the Henry rifle up to me. It was a long, heavy rifle with an octagonal barrel and full-length magazine. The old, dark stock was scarred and oil stained. Chase Malone shoved his Winchester into the saddle scabbard, and mounted.

"Can you carry that big old rifle?" he asked.

"I think so."

"Carry it Indian style — crossways in front of you," he said. "Keep the business end pointed away from me. That's it. Balance it across the pommel."

We rode across the flat grassland of the Sweetwater Valley toward the red cliffs. The sun was down, but the light was good. The sky was still sunlighted, deep blue in color. We rode into the scattered sagebrush clumps that lined the edge of the valley at the base of the red cliffs.

We dismounted. I watched Chase Malone stick a dozen tin cans on the tips of sagebrush. We backed away thirty or forty yards and tied the horses. Chase Malone started to explain how I should hold the big Henry rifle in the natural pocket of my right shoulder.

"I'm left-handed," I said.

"That's right," he said. "I noticed that when you were hammering staples this afternoon. It doesn't matter a bit. One of the best marksmen I ever knew in the Army was left-handed. Hold the rifle against your left shoulder. Raise your elbow so it sticks almost straight out. Feel the pocket the rifle butt fits into? There's no need to hold the rifle tight. Just hold it snug. Relax. When you fire, your shoulder gives with the kick. Now, sight down the barrel. See that V? Now, look at the bead down on the end of the barrel. Put that little bead down into the V and aim at one of the cans."

The long barrel swayed back and forth, passing by the can I aimed at. I gripped tighter and tried to hold it still. But my arms soon grew tired and I lowered the rifle. Chase Malone took it from me and loaded it. I watched him open the magazine at the end of the barrel and feed in half a dozen rounds. He handed it back to me and told me to work the lever.

The mechanism was well-oiled. When I worked the lever, it made little more noise than two pieces of soap being rubbed together. I caught a glimpse of one of the brass casings being lifted up and shoved into the breech. Chase Malone reminded me not to touch the trigger until I was ready to fire.

"Aim at one of the cans," he said. "Relax and hold old Henry steady — not tight, but steady. A good rifleman is relaxed. Are you aimed? Squeeze down on the trigger. As soon as you feel it tighten, you know you're within a sixteenth of an inch of firing. Feel it?"

I held the bead down in the V of the sight and saw it sway past one of the cans. I squeezed farther back on the trigger and suddenly my ears were filled with a roar and I felt myself shoved backward. I caught my balance and lowered the rifle. The tin can was still there.

"I missed it," I said.

"You sure did," Chase Malone said. "But I was watching you squeeze down on the trigger. You did that right, and that's important. Men who yank back on the trigger miss more than they hit. If you aim steady and squeeze like that, you'll get a hit. Try again."

I worked the lever and brought the Henry to my shoulder, raising my elbow until I felt the rifle butt fit into the pocket. I took aim at the same can. I set the bead down in the V and held the barrel steady. I knew it would start swaying soon, so I squeezed back on the trigger. The Henry punched my shoulder back as the roar filled my ears again.

"You got it!" Chase Malone exclaimed.

I looked through the haze of powder smoke and saw that the can was gone. Chase Malone walked ahead and looked around in the sagebrush. He bent over and came up with the mangled can. He brought it back and handed it to me. The bullet had smashed the can in and torn open the backside, leaving a jagged edge with shining points.

"Shoot that way every time," Chase Malone said, "and you'll be a marksman for sure. That was a dead center shot."

When I raised the rifle the third time, I knew I could hit anything I aimed at. I leveled down on a tin can, squeezed the trigger, and missed. The fifth and sixth shots missed, too. I asked what I was doing wrong. Chase Malone said I was probably holding the rifle too tight which would make the barrel sway back and forth.

"If you try to fire as the sight moves past a target, you'll usually miss your target," he said. "The trick is to be relaxed and steady. Are you feeling tired?"

I nodded. I was tired and discouraged.

"That's enough for today," he said. "We're losing the light."

I watched him load the Winchester with a dozen rounds. When he fired, he fired quickly. The hand that worked the rifle lever was almost a blur. The first two shots missed, but the next ten sent ten cans spinning into the air. Empty brass shell casings flew out of the Winchester and one barely hit the ground before another came down.

"Shoots a little low," he said after the twelfth shot. "I had to aim high to hit anything. I'll have to adjust the sight a notch or two."

My ears were still ringing as I looked from Chase Malone to the sagebrush where the tin cans had been.

I said, "I wish I could shoot that way."

"You will, Boomer," he said, "you will. All it takes is practice. In another week you'll be hitting nine out of ten or better. You watch."

CHAPTER XIII

It was dark by the time I left the saloon that night. Chase Malone had given me a late lesson in cleaning the Henry rifle. Ella must have heard me ride into her yard for she came outside and held the lantern while I unsaddled the pony and turned him out into the corral with Billy and Bobby.

Ella asked me how the shooting had gone. After I told her, she said I shouldn't expect much the first time and not to be discouraged. I would do better tomorrow, she said. But I was tired and afraid I would never do any better.

"White Wolf was here today," Ella said.

"When?"

"This afternoon," she said, "when you and Chase were working on the south fence."

I looked into the shadows cast in her face by the lantern. "Did he see the pony?"

"He saw him," she said, "but he didn't say a thing about him. He stood beside the corral for a while, then he came up to the cabin and drank a cup of coffee and ate a few cookies. Then he up and left. Something was eating on him." Her eyes flickered in the light as they shifted away from me. "Maybe he wasn't feeling good. He may be older than I thought."

I said, "This morning he watched us putting up fence. He didn't act friendly. He wouldn't come down and talk to us. Chase Malone said you won't find a Cheyenne who likes fences. Maybe that's what put him into a mood."

"Maybe," Ella said. She looked out into the corral. The distance faded the lantern light and the three horses looked like shadows. "Well, you'd better get some sleep, Boomer. Tomorrow will be as long as today was."

When I climbed into the bunk in the barn, I felt tired, but all wound up, too. I closed my eyes and saw the bead on the end of the Henry's long barrel swaying around the V of the near sight like a bee around a bright flower. In my mind I tried to bring the bead down into the V and hold it there. But the harder I tried and the tighter I held on, the farther away the bead swayed. I broke into a sweat and my legs began to cramp. I found that my hands had clenched themselves into fists.

I must have finally relaxed and dropped

off to sleep. When I opened my eyes, it was against harsh daylight coming through the open barn door. I heard Ella telling me to get washed up for breakfast.

Outside the sun was up as I washed in the stock trough. I tried to catch my wavy reflection in the water to smooth my hair back. I felt for the beard that was never there.

That morning as I walked across the yard toward the cabin, I got a new look at the place. It was almost like being inside a color picture in a book. The low cabin sat along the edge of the tree line with smoke drifting up from its stovepipe, making a lazy trail to the morning sky. The smell of grass and a faint smell from the corral filled the air. I heard the sounds of bees and flies. And in the cottonwoods birds sang loudly and made short, darting flights from one limb to another.

Inside the cabin Chase Malone sat at the rough pine table with a cup of coffee before him. When I sat down Ella poured me a cup. It steamed up into my face and smelled better than it ever had before.

"Are you ready for another day, Boomer?" Chase Malone asked.

I nodded while I sipped the coffee.

"This afternoon we'll quit early," he

said. "I got to thinking about it last night. Dusk is the hardest time of day to fire a rifle and that was probably why you had a hard time. This afternoon I want you to get some shooting in before the sun goes down. The fence can wait."

I had almost forgotten I'd had a bad time aiming the Henry rifle. That morning I felt like I could pick up the Henry and hit anything I aimed at. Ella served up a breakfast of eggs, bacon, and cornbread. I'd never felt so hungry. Ella and Chase Malone had finished eating, but I was starting on my third square of cornbread with honey.

"Hungriest boy I ever saw," Chase Malone said.

Ella smiled at me. "What are you so happy about, Boomer?"

I shrugged and kept my mouth full so I wouldn't have to say anything.

"You sure must be happy about something," Ella said. "There's been a big smile on your face from the time I woke you up and now you're eating everything in sight."

I shrugged again.

"Hell," Chase Malone growled, "I told you yesterday what was wrong with him. He's in love with Birdy."

I felt my face grow hot as I looked down

at my empty breakfast plate.

Ella stood and gathered up the dishes. "Now, Chase, don't you be rawhiding him all day. He might up and quit. Then where would you be?"

"You're right," Chase Malone said, rising from his chair. "I can't get along without him until we finish the south fence — and until he beefs that locoed steer." He winked at me. "But after that, watch out."

As we drove down the valley that morning I watched the tree line where White Wolf's camp was. Chase Malone saw the smoke above the trees and said if White Wolf kept burning fuel that way, he would have to move his camp before long. I wanted to get him talking about the Indian girl again, but I didn't want to ask him outright.

I told Chase Malone what Ella said to me last night about White Wolf coming up to the cabin and being in a mood of some kind. "Maybe you could talk to him and find out what's wrong."

Chase Malone shook his head. "If White Wolf has something to say to us, he'll say it. But if he's not talking, then there's no sense in wasting breath on him."

I couldn't think of a way to get him to talk about the Indian girl, so I let it go. But as we dug post holes that morning, I kept watching for her. I studied the shadows back in the cottonwood grove, hoping to see something move. A few times I thought I saw movement, but I was never sure. Each fence post we put in took us farther away from the trees and by noon we were so far away that I gave up watching.

Not long after the middle of the afternoon we stopped work and went to the firing range, as Chase Malone called the area near the red cliffs where we shot at tin cans. I made three hits with my first three shots. It was so easy that I wondered how I'd ever missed last evening. But my fourth and fifth shots missed, the sixth nicked a can and sent it spinning, and the next three shots were all solid hits.

Chase Malone was as excited as I was. "You're doing everything right, Boomer! You're holding old Henry snug and you're squeezing the trigger slow and easy. You keep on this way and you never will miss!"

I stepped back while Chase Malone aimed his Winchester. He'd adjusted the rear sight last night to correct it from shooting low. I was swelled with pride at my own shooting and with Chase Malone's praise, but when he fired the Winchester, I was quickly humbled. He worked the lever with blazing speed and never missed a shot. Cans flew off the sagebrush and spun into the air like flushed birds amid the roar of firing.

A thick and heavy silence closed around us when he lowered the rifle. In disbelief I looked at the profile of his face, the side of one bulging eye that made the man look so intense, and the wild growth of hair that threatened to throw his hat off his head.

"This is the best rifle I ever owned," he said. He glanced at me and I saw an expression of mild surprise and pleasure in his face. I was still too amazed to say anything. I'd seen him fire quickly last evening, but that had been nothing compared to this. His accuracy was deadly and final. And despite myself, I felt frightened.

Chase Malone must have seen some of my thoughts on my face when he looked at me again. For he said, "A rifle like this makes a man want to show off."

But I knew then that no matter how good a rifleman I was to become, I would never be as good as Chase Malone. His shooting went beyond skill. It was as close to perfection as any I ever hoped to see. I remembered when we had been in town and I'd stopped the buckboard in the street along Saloon Row to look back at Sheriff

Hobbs as he walked toward Chase Malone. I could feel then that something was about to happen. But even after I saw it, after I saw Hobbs back down from Chase Malone and walk backward like an actor in a comedy play, I didn't understand all of it. I did now.

That evening we sat on the front edge of the saloon porch and cleaned the two rifles.

"You learn fast," Chase Malone said, as I was wiping the cleaned rifle with an oily rag.

I said, "My father used to say that left-handed people weren't as good at doing things as right-handers."

"Where did he get that idea?"

"I don't know," I said. "From me, I guess."

"Why?"

"I'm always doing things wrong."

"I haven't seen you do anything wrong since you landed here," Chase Malone said.

"I did wrong when I got lost," I said. "My mare died because of it."

Chase Malone laid the Winchester across his knees and said, "You know more about that than I do, Boomer. But one thing you'll learn as you get older is that we all make mistakes and we have to live with them. Sometimes we can undo a mistake and make up for it, but usually we can't. You can't bring that mare back to life, no matter what you do. The best you can do is to admit the mistake and try not to make it again. I'll tell you one thing: if riding your mare into the ground is the worst mistake you ever make, then you'll be better off than most men." He paused and added, "You don't like your father much, do you?"

To avoid Chase Malone's eyes, I looked down at the Henry rifle in my hands. The blued metal gleamed dully in the evening light. I shook my head.

"I don't aim to pry into your business, Boomer, but let me tell you something. When I was sixteen or seventeen, I didn't think much of my father, either. For one thing he didn't know a damn thing — at least he didn't know the things I thought were worth knowing. I wanted to run off and join the Army of the West. That was my life's dream. But my father was a practical man and he made me stay home and go to school. I went into his profession when I was twenty-one. The next year I married a woman who had my father's approval.

221

"But after a few years I went into the Army and started my life over again. But that's another story. What I wanted to tell you is that when I took my first furlough I went home and saw my father. I felt like a visitor in that house where I'd grown up. My father looked old to me, old and frail. He asked me how I was getting along and was I making my own way. I says, 'Yes, sir.' 'Well,' he says to me, 'that's what counts. You may yet make your mark.'

"Then we stood up and shook hands like a couple of distant relatives might, and he showed me to the door. That was the last time I ever saw him. He died the following winter. But he had come as close to forgiving me as he could and I respected him for that. I've always regretted that I never told him so."

"Forgive you for what?" I asked.

"For throwing away the career he had chosen for me — and the woman."

"But why did you?"

"It was something I had to do, Boomer. I knew I would always be restless and unhappy until I did. I wish I had done it sooner. A man who doesn't follow his lights can never be happy. I say a man can get educated any time, but he's only young once. That's the time for him to get out and see things and explore new country — like you're doing. I wish I'd done it your way."

Chase Malone fell silent and looked out across the valley. Neither of us spoke in the gathering darkness until Chase Malone said I should head back for the cabin.

He handed the Henry rifle and a box of ammunition up to me after I'd climbed up into the saddle.

"You might as well start carrying old Henry," he said.

A wave of excitement ran through me. "But it's your rifle."

"I can only shoot one at a time," he said. "You can have this one on loan."

He touched the pony's face with his fingertips. "When are you going to wash that red stuff off?"

"Ella said I should leave it on for two or three weeks," I said. "What do you think?"

"As long as it doesn't bother him I reckon it's all right." He laughed. "It's the craziest thing I ever heard of."

"Do you think it'll work?"

He shrugged. "Probably will. From a distance you'd think this was just another roan pony." He ran his hand down the pony's shoulder. "This is a good-natured horse. He's calm and easygoing. I noticed the gunfire didn't bother him much. And he acts like he knows who you are."

"I feed him myself and comb him out every day."

"Do you think he's ready for a long ride?"

Without thinking, I said, "I wish I had time to take him on a long ride."

Chase Malone laughed. "You talk like Ella and I are working you to death. Well, you may have your chance for a good ride. In another day or two I may want you to go to town for me."

"To Sunbonnet?"

He nodded, smiling. "If you think this cayuse can walk that far."

"Oh, he can," I said.

Chase Malone laughed and waved me away. "I'll see you at breakfast, Boomer."

I rode down the valley to the cabin, smelling wood smoke from the cookstove before I was in sight of it. Ella had supper ready. She met me at the door after I'd turned the pony into the corral.

"It's been a long time since I've heard any shooting," she said. "Where have you been all this time?"

"We got to talking," I said. "Chase Malone told me about his life before he came out here." I leaned the rifle up in a corner near the door.

"Did Chase Malone give that to you?" she asked.

"He gave it to me on loan."

"You must be on mighty good terms with Chase," she said as we sat down to eat. "I didn't think he'd loan that old rifle to anybody. And he sure as hell never talks about his growing-up days to me. What did he tell you?"

I shrugged. I didn't know what to say to her. Chase Malone had spoken to me as he might to another man and somehow it didn't seem right that I should repeat it. It was between the two of us.

Ella said, "I have a feeling I shouldn't have asked that."

"There's nothing to tell," I said.

"You men," Ella said. Then she asked, "How did your shooting go today?"

"Better," I said. "But mine was nothing compared to Chase Malone's."

"You can't expect to be that good," Ella said. "Chase has a fair reputation with a rifle."

"Fair," I said. "He must be the best."

Ella smiled. "He might be. He just might be."

After we cleaned up the dishes and pans that night, I told her that Chase Malone had asked me to ride into town for him in another day or two. Ella was surprised.

"He didn't say why," I said. I hadn't thought to ask. All I'd been able to think about was riding the pony all the way to Sunbonnet and back by myself.

Before I went to bed that night I made a careful search of the barn. I even took the lantern up into the loft and looked around there. Satisfied that the barn was empty, I walked back up the runway.

CHAPTER XIV

After two more days of working on the fence and after two late afternoons on the firing range, I was violently awakened on the morning I was to ride to Sunbonnet. The Indian girl shook me awake at dawn, sobbing miserably, and motioning for me to come with her.

I saw blood on the front of her buckskin dress. I leaped out of the bunk, thinking she was hurt. But she brushed me away when I reached for her. I realized the blood was not hers, but had been splattered on her.

She watched me and sobbed while I yanked on my boots, then she snatched the Henry from where I had leaned it against the wall of the barn, shoved it into my hands, and ran.

She was fast. I ran after her down the barn's runway, out the back door, through the corral, and into the trees. The air was cool and fragrant in the gray light of morning. I followed the running Indian girl into a stand of willows that slapped my legs. I caught a glimpse of her as she ran

227

between two trees, her braids bouncing against her back and her moccasins flashing.

My breath was coming hard when I ran between the two cottonwoods. I'd lost her. I slowed, looking from side to side, and then I heard a sorrowful wailing ahead, a mourning sound that raised and lowered in pitch. I ran through the trees toward the wailing and soon realized I was near the brush corral in White Wolf's camp. Then I saw it.

I came around the corral at a full run, almost knowing what I would see and filled with the desperate thought that it was too late. I found the old squaw on her knees beside the smoky fire. She wailed pitifully. White Wolf lay stretched out before her, his middle covered with bright, flowing blood. A big pool of blood beside him glistened in the early morning light.

I thought he must be dead. But an instant before the Indian girl shrieked at me, I saw his chest heave.

The girl stood in the trees between the corral and the open valley. She screamed over the sounds of the old squaw's wailing, waving for me to follow her. When I took a step toward her, she turned and ran for the valley.

I came out of the trees on the run and saw the Indian girl pointing at a Cheyenne brave not more than fifty yards away. His savage, painted face was turned toward us and he sat his pony as still as a wild animal caught in the open. Behind him were White Wolf's two squaws. Each was mounted on a spotted pony, and each led another pony. I remembered then that the brush corral had been empty.

Though I couldn't understand the Indian girl's words, I knew what her gestures meant, what she wanted me to do. I levered a round into the Henry rifle and brought it to my shoulder. I held the sights steady and lined the bead on the brave's painted face.

He stared back at me, motionless, and without fear. His expression was one of savage fierceness that I had never seen in a man. The Indian girl had become suddenly quiet and the only sounds I heard over my pounding heart were the wails of the old squaw.

I lowered the rifle and my eyes fell away from the brave's stare. The girl began shrieking at me again. I looked up and saw the Cheyenne warrior knee his pony and ride out through the tall grass. The two squaws followed close behind.

The Indian girl threw herself at me, but I dodged her. She fell into the grass and lay there, screaming. I started to run back into the grove of trees, but then I changed my mind and ran up the valley to the cabin.

Ella had just gotten out of bed. I quickly told her what had happened. She put on her traveling duster over her nightgown, grabbed a tin box, and we half ran and half walked back to White Wolf's camp. The sun was coming up. The eastern sky was as red as blood.

White Wolf hadn't moved. Neither had the wailing squaw. I had never imagined there was so much blood inside a man. The red pool beside him looked even bigger than before and I thought he could not be alive. But as Ella squatted beside him and began to cut away his buckskin shirt with a pair of scissors from the tin box, I saw White Wolf's chest heave with surprising strength.

The squaw wailed as Ella mopped blood from White Wolf's chest. The Indian girl stood some distance away, sobbing as she watched White Wolf. She wouldn't look at me.

"You can stop that racket any time," Ella said to the whitehaired squaw. "He ain't going to die right this minute." As though the woman understood, she suddenly stopped wailing. Then I heard White Wolf's rough breathing.

Ella wrapped his chest with a wide bandage and tied it tight. Blood seeped through, but it was not flowing as it had been. Ella's white duster was splattered with drying blood. Her hands looked like they had been dipped in red paint.

Ella said, "Boomer, find a pot or something and bring some water up from the river. I need to wash him down to make sure he doesn't have any more holes in him."

I found a clay jug near the edge of the corral and filled it with water. Ella used a rag to wipe down White Wolf's bare chest. His breathing was even now, almost calm. His eyes were open and he blinked up at the sky.

Ella spoke in a soothing voice: "Tough old bastard, ain't you? Why did you let some young buck sneak in here and carve on you? I thought you had everything figured out. Getting careless in your old age, ain't you?"

White Wolf looked at her, but he didn't answer. Ella sat back and I saw her relax. Her face was shiny with sweat. She wiped it with the sleeve of her duster. When she looked up, she saw the Indian girl.

"What the hell's wrong with her?" Ella asked. "She looks worse than this old squaw."

"She wanted me to shoot that Indian," I said. "I aimed at him. I had him in the sights just like a tin can. I was even squeezing down on the trigger."

"But you stopped."

I nodded. "I don't know why. I just did."

"You're no killer, that's why," Ella said. Then she added, "It wasn't your fight. You were smart to stay out of it."

"But I'm a part of it," I said. "That warrior only wanted his horse. If he'd found him, he might have taken him and left."

"No," Ella said impatiently, "none of this was your doing. You didn't ask for that pony. I even tried to talk White Wolf out of it, remember? He knew what he was up against when he stole that pony."

"I'm going to give him back," I said.

"The hell you are," Ella said. "White Wolf would never forgive you if you did. You know how he thinks of you. You're supposed to be the boy he's seen in his visions. He thinks he has to look out for you. If you take that away from him, he'll never forgive you."

I spent all morning with Ella as she

nursed White Wolf. I made one trip back to the cabin and brought some medicine and a spoon back for Ella. She made White Wolf take three different kinds of medicine. After taking the last kind he gathered up the strength to push the spoon away. He lay back and closed his eyes.

It was noon by the sun when Ella and I walked back up to the cabin. The sky was clear and the air was still as we walked along the wagon ruts, stepping on our short shadows.

"Say, didn't Chase want you to ride into town today?" Ella asked.

I nodded grimly. I didn't know why, but I felt worn out.

"Well, it's too late in the day for you to start out now," Ella said. "You wait and go in the morning. All Chase wanted was a copy of the newspaper so he could see if Cotton Turner got his letter spelled right."

Even though I was tired I still wanted to go to Sunbonnet that day. I'd been planning on it ever since Chase Malone first told me. Once you get your mouth set on a thing, it's hard to swallow. And I knew if I hurried I could make it to town and back by dark. But I would have to push the pony to do it, and even as I thought it, I knew I would never be able to push a horse again after what happened to Pepper.

"I'll leave in the morning," I said.

"Chase will understand," Ella said, putting her arm around me as we walked.

We found Chase Malone waiting for us at the cabin. Ella explained to him what had happened. I saw him look at the Henry rifle in my hand.

Chase Malone said, "From the look of you I'd have guessed Boomer was using you for target practice. Only I thought he was a better shot."

Ella looked down at herself, then a hand moved to her tangled hair. "I do look like hell, don't I? You two stay out here while this critter makes herself into a woman again."

Chase Malone went out to the corral with me and watched while I fed the horses and combed out the pony.

"You can scrub his face now, I reckon," Chase Malone said.

I stopped currying and looked at the pony. I hadn't thought of that. I said I would ask Ella what would be the best way to do it. I would sure be glad to see his head white like it was supposed to be.

"Have you thought of a name for that cayuse yet, Boomer?" Chase Malone asked.

I went back to currying the pony. His roan coat was beginning to gleam in the sun. "White Wolf."

"What?" Chase Malone asked.

"I'm going to name him White Wolf," I said.

"Funny name for a horse," he said. "But it fits, I reckon." After a silence he asked, "How bad was White Wolf cut?"

"I don't know," I said. "But it looked bad. He bled all over the place."

"I wonder how he let that buck get to him," Chase Malone said. "I may walk down there this afternoon and see what I can find out. Are you going to town for me tomorrow?"

I nodded. "I was going in this afternoon, but Ella said I should wait."

"There's no hurry," Chase Malone said. "Pick me up a copy of the latest paper as well as the one with my letter in it. Give Cotton Turner some hell for me."

Ella called us for dinner and during the meal Chase Malone said that we would take a day off from working on the fence.

Ella said, "I want you two men to come down to White Wolf's camp and carry him to his tepee this afternoon. We can't leave him laying out in the open all night."

"How bad off is he?" Chase Malone asked.

"I won't know for another day or two," Ella said. "That brave sure buried a knife in him, I'll tell you that."

When the three of us walked back to the brush corral, White Wolf was gone. We followed a trail of blood through the brush that led toward the river. White Wolf had dragged himself back to his tepee. Angrily, Ella threw open the flap and ducked inside, cursing. I was carrying the tin box.

Ella said to me, "Boomer, give me another one of those wide bandages and the goddam scissors. The chief of the Cheyenne is bleeding like a stuck hog."

I squatted down before the opening and handed her a bandage and the pair of scissors. In a minute she threw out a blood-soaked bandage. I didn't know how she could see what she was doing. As I looked inside, I could see Ella's dim form as she leaned over White Wolf. I saw another form deeper in the tepee that I took to be the Indian girl. She was too slender to be the old squaw.

Ella came out of the tepee, a disgusted look on her face. "That old bastard will kill himself yet."

"He probably thinks he's dying," Chase

Malone said. "A man wants to die in his home."

"Well, that's about what's going to happen," Ella said. Then her shoulders shook and she sobbed. "Christ, I had some hope until now." She stepped into Chase Malone's arms.

"He's been through worse than this," Chase Malone said.

Ella stepped back and dried her eyes on the sleeve of her gingham dress. Her voice was choked when she said, "He's been younger, too."

Chase Malone went inside the tepee. I heard him speaking in a low, guttural voice. Then I heard the Indian girl. They talked for quite a while as I sat beside the opening.

When Chase Malone came outside, he looked at me and grinned crookedly. "Birdy has a low opinion of you, Boomer."

Ella said, "She's crazy. You know that. She should never have let White Wolf move."

"Indian women do what they're told," Chase Malone said dryly. "I found out what happened. That Cheyenne brave walked right into the trap White Wolf set for him. Only White Wolf tried to use that old revolver and it misfired. That's how the brave was able to get a knife into him. Birdy says white man's medicine isn't worth a damn. She took the revolver and threw it in the river before she came after Boomer. She thinks you didn't shoot that brave because you were afraid the rifle wouldn't work."

"She don't know up from down," Ella said. "Let's get out of here. I can't take any more of this Indian business. You try to help them and what does it get you?"

"The Cheyenne have their own ways, Ella," Chase Malone said. "You aren't going to change them."

Ella shook her head as she looked into the dark opening of the tepee. "You're right, Chase. I reckon I shouldn't be trying to."

We walked back to the cabin. I caught the pony and snubbed him down while Ella scrubbed his face with soapy water. Some of the soap must have run into his eyes because he about wore himself out trying to get loose. But when Ella was done, the pony's head was white as a cloud.

I turned him loose and when he got his wind, he bucked and sunfished and galloped around the corral, looking for a way out.

Chase Malone laughed and said, "Saddle him up and take him for a ride, Boomer."

"I believe I'll let him cool off a little," I said.

"Ain't he pretty?" Ella said. "I've never seen such a beautiful pony, have you?"

"Can't say I have," Chase Malone agreed. "But you're going to have to butter him up more than that to get him over being mad."

"He'll get over it," Ella said.

Later in the afternoon he did get over it. I threw a saddle on him and rode him around the corral for a while, guiding him with a hackamore. Then I opened the gate and rode him out into the grass. He pitched a couple of times, but I knew he wasn't trying to throw me.

I rode him across the grassland of the valley, down to the south boundary marked by an even line of fence posts stretching from the trees almost all the way to the wagon ruts. The cattle had drifted south and were grazing. I circled around them and drove a bunch back up north. They spread out in front of me and tried to circle back. The pony caught on to the game fast and moved to the side to keep them headed.

Then I remembered One Eye and wished I'd brought the Henry rifle. I rode into a draw spotted with sagebrush and tangled with weeds that led through a break in the red cliffs. The air was hot and still as though I had ridden inside a tin can. I heard the buzzing of insects, then the pony shied and backed up. Movement on the ground caught my eye and I saw a brown spotted snake coiling in front of us. I'd never seen a rattler before, but when he buzzed his warning, I knew that's what he was. The pony snorted and pawed dirt. I turned him and rode out of the draw. It was foolish to be looking for One Eye when I wasn't carrying the rifle. What if he had been back in the draw and had charged?

I rode back across the valley, feeling lucky that the worst had not happened and feeling good about the pony, White Wolf. Thinking of the name, I looked at the tree line near White Wolf's camp, the memory of the bloody, frightening morning crowding back into my mind. It took me a while to see what was different about the tree line. The haze from the smoky fire was not there.

CHAPTER XV

I rode down the valley at sunup the next morning, alone and happy to be going. The pony pranced and bobbed his pure white head with excitement. I wondered if he felt the same quivering in his stomach that I felt in mine.

But as I passed the tree line near the Indian camp, I wondered if White Wolf had lived through the night. I'd been afraid to ask Ella that morning. I knew she feared the worst. I'd decided to wait until I came back from town to ask her. She would know by then.

By lamplight Ella had packed a lunch for me. From the cowhide trunk she dug out a yellow slicker that I wrapped around the lunch and tied on the cantle. Ella fretted around like a hen and kept asking me if there was anything else I needed as if I was going away for a week. Then at dawn I'd mounted up and ridden to the front of the cabin. Ella came out carrying her big make-up case.

"Can you tie this on behind?" she asked.

I stepped down. Ella added softly, "I want you to give it back to Coralee. You won't mind, will you?"

I had ridden all the way to the south end of the valley before I remembered something that made me understand why Ella was returning her make-up case to Coralee. Coralee had said that as long as Ella kept it, it meant she wasn't burning any bridges, that she could always come back. Ella had replied that she would not come back. Now, I guessed, she was proving it.

I rode out of the valley into the open desert. The sun was up, casting its bright light on the sagebrush and sticker weeds. The early sun gave my pony a long shadow, topped by someone wearing a six-foot Stetson.

For the first time I saw some green in the desert. The low, curled grass that I thought must always be brown was now showing new green spikes. Spring had been in the Sweetwater Valley for some time, but it was only now bringing life to the high desert.

My stomach was rumbling with hunger by midmorning. I reined up and stepped down to stretch my legs. While the pony sniffed the new grass, I unwrapped my lunch from the slicker. I planned to eat only the two squares of cornbread that Ella had put in the lunch, but they didn't come near to filling me up. I ended up eating the whole lunch and wishing there was more.

I wrapped the yellow slicker around the make-up case and strapped it to the cantle. When I mounted up and glanced at the sun, I guessed the time to be only nine o'clock. I clucked the pony into a trot and was only thinking about letting him run when he broke into a gallop. I tugged my hat down on my head and let him go.

Then I felt the cornbread, cold meat, and water coming back up the same route they had gone down. I reined the pony down to a walk. He looked back at me as though to say, "What's wrong with a boy who won't let his horse run?"

It was late morning by the time I crossed the railroad tracks and turned onto the main road. Ahead I saw the water tower. The pony shied at the bridge that crossed the Sweetwater River, and I finally had to dismount and lead him across.

In town I rode straight for MacRae's Livery and let the pony drink from the trough. I rinsed my face and arms with the cool water and this time I had my own bandanna handkerchief to dry myself with.

MacRae had stepped out in front of his shop and was watching me. He wore a long leather apron. I felt a little foolish then, realizing I was only copying what I had done when I'd come to town with Chase Malone. A man doesn't get near as dusty riding a horse as he does sitting behind a team.

MacRae took off his apron and walked over to me, looking at the pony. "How old is he?"

"I don't know," I said.

MacRae took a long glance at me, then walked around the pony, expertly running his hand over his sides and flanks. He lifted the pony's head and pulled his lip up. "Injun war pony. Cheyenne. How did you get ahold of him, boy?"

When I didn't answer, MacRae looked at me and smiled in a friendly way. "I ain't asking for a bill of sale, mind you. I'm just curious. A man doesn't see a horse like this one every day."

I smiled back at MacRae, but I felt uncomfortable.

"I might buy him if I knew you had a price on him."

"I'd never sell him," I said.

"Can't say I blame you," MacRae said, stepping back from the pony. "You might think about getting his hoofs trimmed and having him shod."

I took the pony's reins and started to turn him to head across the street.

MacRae said, "Seems like I've seen you somewhere."

"I was in town with Chase Malone a while back," I said.

"Oh, sure," he said, "that's right. Are you bunked up there on the Sweetwater?"

I nodded. "I'm hired out to Ella and Chase Malone."

"You are, eh?"

"Chase Malone and I are putting in a fence. He wants to keep his stock from drifting."

"That's wise," MacRae said soberly. "Anybody else camped up there in that valley?"

"No," I said. "But people might be living up there someday — homesteaders."

"Maybe," he said. MacRae curled his lips together, turned his head and spat a long stream of tobacco juice into the corral. It shot out of his mouth like a thin, shining snake. "Aw, there's a powerful lot of hard talk going around about Malone these days."

When he looked at me, I knew he was sizing me up to find out if I had any idea what he was talking about.

I said, "Reese Clarke is trying to run us out of the Sweetwater Valley. He's been writing lies about Chase Malone."

MacRae smiled as if I'd given him the answer he wanted. "There's one thing for sure: With Malone and that woman, Ella, Reese Clarke has a tall job of work in front of him."

"They aren't going to be run off," I said.

MacRae laughed out loud. "If that's what Malone says, then I believe it. Say what you want about Chase Malone, but, by God, he's a man of his word." He started toward the door of the livery, then turned back and said, "If you change your mind about selling that Injun horse, let me know."

I led my pony across the street. The water wagon had rolled by while I was talking with MacRae. As I walked, my boots scuffed away a layer of damp dirt, uncovering the dust underneath. I tied the pony to the tie rail in front of the Sunbonnet *Global News* building and stepped up on the boardwalk in front of the big plate-glass window.

Cotton Turner met me at the door, extending his ink-stained hand. "Well, am I glad to see you, Boomer."

I was surprised by his eager friendliness, and pleased that he remembered my name. We shook hands.

"Did you bring that other outlaw with you?" Cotton Turner grinned so that his teeth showed through his beard.

"I rode in alone," I said. "Chase Malone wants me to pick up a copy of the paper that had his letter in it. He wants yesterday's, too."

"That can be arranged," Cotton Turner said. He looked back into his office. It was dark and gloomy in there. I saw the dark shape of a press deep inside. Even standing in the open doorway I could smell newsprint and printer's ink.

Cotton Turner drew out his pocket watch and snapped open the cover. "I'm at a good stopping place. It's a mite early, but I'll stand you to a lunch if you think you could eat."

"No, sir," I said. "I mean, it isn't too early for me. I can eat."

Cotton Turner laughed. "I thought so." He pulled the door shut, locked it with a skeleton key, and we walked down the boardwalk to the Sunbonnet House.

I followed the editor through the hotel lobby and into the nearly empty dining room. He went to the same table by the window where he'd been sitting when I'd first met him. The same redheaded waitress served us. She traded strange remarks with Cotton Turner again. She filled our cups with mud and brought a wicker basket of "adobe" bread. The Special-of-the-Day was stew again. The waitress called it "plaid stew." Cotton Turner asked her to marry him.

"Anything's possible," the redheaded waitress answered.

"Nothing's impossible," Cotton Turner said.

The waitress giggled and left, rustling her starched dress. I wondered if the two of them went through that every day.

We ate in silence, but after the meal Cotton Turner said he had something serious to tell me, something Chase Malone should know about.

"Yesterday a C Bar rider delivered another of Reese Clarke's tirades to be published in the *Global News*."

"His other letter was full of lies," I said.

"This one may be, too," Cotton Turner said, "but you can bet a lot of folks believe what he says. He's a respected man in this territory."

"Chase Malone told me that, too."

Cotton Turner nodded. "In this new

letter Reese Clarke claims that Malone and Ella are living together in sin. He says they're stealing money from the local cowboys in games of chance."

"That's not true," I said.

"There is one other thing that's a little rougher," the editor said. "He accuses Chase Malone of dealing in stolen cattle. He says Chase doesn't have a registered brand. That way he doesn't have to admit his stock is stolen. He can say the cattle drifted into the valley from neighboring ranches. Clarke says that if Chase Malone was an honest man, he would have a brand listed in the registry." Cotton Turner looked at me.

"I don't know if he has one or not," I said.

"I don't, either," Cotton Turner said. "I wish I did. I sent a wire yesterday to the Cattleman's Association in Cheyenne. I hope to hear from them this afternoon or tomorrow morning. Boomer, I want you to tell Chase about this latest accusation. If he can't come up with a good answer to this one, he's in hot water. It just doesn't look right for a man to run cattle without owning a brand — no matter how many bills of sale he can produce. You tell that to Chase."

"I will," I said.

"Well, come on back to the shop and I'll give you those papers," Cotton Turner said.

We were outside, walking along the boardwalk, when he asked me, "Is Reese Clarke hiring Texans to run his errands these days?"

"I don't know," I said. "Why?"

"The rider who delivered Clarke's letter to me was dressed up brighter than a bride on Saturday. Why, I haven't seen anybody like him, or heard anybody talk like him, since the herds used to come up to the railhead in Nebraska years back. And when I looked outside the shop there was another one just like him, only younger. I don't know why it took two men to deliver a letter." He laughed. "One to carry it, one to guard the carrier?"

I thought he had probably seen the same young cowboy who had been with the ones who came after Buck that night. He had laughed loud and dressed in flashy clothes.

Inside the newspaper office Cotton Turner gave me a copy of the paper that had Chase Malone's letter and a copy of yesterday's paper.

As I left, he said to me, "Be sure to deliver that message to Chase."

250

"I will," I said. "Thanks for the lunch, Mr. Turner."

"You call me Cotton. Stop by anytime, Boomer."

I walked out of the office and missed running into Mrs. Skinner by an inch. I apologized and touched my hand to my hat. She took a long look at me and walked on. I knew she was trying to place me. I stuffed the two newspapers inside my shirt and was untying my pony from the tie rail when I heard a hissing sound behind me.

I turned and saw the pinched face of Mrs. Skinner. Her mouth scowled at me and her sharp elbows were tucked against her sides like sheathed weapons.

"You run off from that Malone," she said in a low voice.

I didn't know if she was asking me or telling me. I shook my head and stepped back.

"Malone is evil, boy," Mrs. Skinner hissed. She came toward me, hunched over. The pony snorted and bobbed his head. "You run off, hear? Malone is evil, sent by the devil."

The pony whinnied then and reared. Mrs. Skinner drew back and looked at the horse in fear. She turned and quickly stepped back up on the boardwalk. She looked at me as though I was trying to kill her, then walked away, her lace-up shoes making pecking sounds on the wood.

The water wagon came by then and the pony decided he should be afraid of that, too, even though he had seen it before. His eyes rolled and he reared again.

I spoke to him and calmed him before mounting up. He was skitterish as I rode down the main street and turned at the intersection that led across the tracks. Standing in the shade of the bank building, across the street from the Sunbonnet House, I saw a familiar figure watching me: Sheriff Hobbs.

I didn't speak to him or even nod as I turned the corner and rode past him. I felt his eyes on me. Once again a fear crept up in me that my father might have sent out a circular about me. A man like Hobbs probably had nothing better to do than to study the posters that came into his office and stand on street corners, looking for rewards to collect.

I rode down saloon row. It was noon by the sun. I passed the Shoofly and saw three men sitting near the batwing doors. The man who was whittling looked up at me. His battered hat was shoved back on his head. I recognized Jake. From the way he looked at me I thought he remembered me and I raised a hand to him. But then I realized he was looking at my pony. He waved in a half-hearted way and went back to his whittling.

Coralee herself answered my knock on the door of the pink house. She started to say something, then she looked me over and her eyes stopped on the make-up case in my hand.

"Goddammit," she said.

"Ella sent me to give this back to you," I said.

"I can see that," she snapped. "I ain't blind. You tell Ella I ain't going to accept it. You just take it on back and tell her that."

"She told me not to come back with it," I lied. "I'll have to leave it here on the porch."

"Oh, give it to me," she said. "What was your name, boy?"

"Boomer."

"I see you edging away, Boomer," she said. "Well, go ahead and go. I can't stop you. Everybody leaves me sooner or later, anyway. You go on. You tell Ella I said thank you for returning this make-up outfit, but that don't mean she can't never come back. You understand my meaning?"

I nodded and started down the porch steps.

"And you say I said thank you!"

I waved at her and closed the gate of the pink fence behind me. I was quite a ways up the street when the door slammed shut, making the pony hop nervously. I passed the Shoofly. Jake was still there, whittling. I turned the corner and crossed the tracks on the sheet that led to the main intersection.

I glanced at the shady side of the bank building, half expecting to see Sheriff Hobbs still standing there. But he was gone. As I turned the corner, a figure caught my eye near the doorway of the Sunbonnet House. Sheriff Hobbs lounged there, watching me ride through town.

Our eyes met for an instant. I looked away, remembering something Chase Malone had said when we had been in town the first time: "Can you top these city folks?" Riding past *SKINNER CLOTHING* and past the hardware store, I rubbed the pony's neck and asked him that.

CHAPTER XVI

I rode right into the rainstorm. A thunderhead hung over the Sweetwater Valley that I saw from far away. I watched sheets of rain and flashes of lightning and heard the rumbling thunder long before I felt the first pelting drops on the shoulders of my slicker. By the time I rode through the break in the rocks that opened into the river crossing and the valley, a stream of water was running off the front of my hatbrim.

The Sweetwater River was running mud. The pony crossed it and then followed the wagon ruts up the valley at a quick pace. We both knew the protection of the barn was less than an hour away.

I would never have seen the two riders if it hadn't been for a flash of lightning followed close by thunder. I looked up at the cliffs, thinking I might see where it had hit. On top of the red cliffs, farther ahead, two yellow shapes caught my eye. They were cast against the black sky, and I knew they were two riders wearing slickers like mine.

They sat their horses on the horizon, still, overlooking Ella's cabin.

I rode the pony into the barn, unsaddled him and wiped him down with a couple of burlap sacks. After I grained him I made a run for the cabin, looking up through the rain at the cliffs where I'd seen the riders. They were gone.

Ella met me with a cup of steaming coffee and a plate of cookies.

"Is White Wolf still alive?" I asked.

She smiled. "I'll bet you've been thinking about him all day, haven't you? Two hours ago he was sound asleep. I heard the storm coming then, so I came back here."

"Do you think he'll make it?"

Ella nodded. "The bleeding stopped. If he makes it through tomorrow, I think he'll be all right."

"I saw two riders up on the cliffs."

Ella had poured herself a cup of coffee and sat down at the table with me. "What were they doing?"

"I don't know. Just sitting up there, looking down here."

Ella smiled. "In the rain?"

I nodded.

"I've heard about folks like that," she said. "Well, tell me about your trip. How did the pony do?"

"Fine," I said. "I gave your make-up case to Coralee. She said to say thank you. Cotton Turner bought me a dinner at the Sunbonnet House."

"Dinner?" Ella said. "What happened to the lunch I packed for you?"

"I ate it."

Ella shook her head. "You sure can eat."

"Cotton Turner gave me the newspapers Chase Malone wanted. He said Reese Clarke wrote another letter to be published. It'll be in tomorrow's paper. He accused Chase Malone of not having a registered brand. Cotton Turner wanted me to be sure to tell him that. Is it true?"

Ella nodded grimly. "Chase applied for a brand almost two years ago. The Cattleman's Association won't allow it. Chase believes Reese Clarke is behind it."

"Cotton Turner said it doesn't look right for a man to own cattle without putting a brand on them."

"He's right," Ella said. "But what else is Chase to do?"

I finished my coffee. "When it stops raining, I'll take the papers up to him."

"Ask him if he wants to come down for supper," Ella said. "When you tell him about Clarke's letter, he'll probably want someone to talk to."

"Reese Clarke said you and Chase Malone were living in sin," I said. "What does that mean?"

Ella smiled. "It means we'd be living together without being married."

"Well, why aren't you married?" I asked. "Are you in love with Buck Stone?"

Ella laughed. "You're full of questions today, aren't you?"

"I'm sorry," I said. "I ought to mind my own business."

"I'll tell you, Boomer," Ella said, "Chase Malone and I aren't married because neither one of us is the kind who could stick it out. We wouldn't be happy under the same roof for long. Don't ask me why that is because I don't know. I only know it's true. And when you ask me if I'm in love with Buck, you hit a sore spot. Buck Stone is a lot of man — like you're going to be."

That embarrassed me and I was glad when Ella changed the subject.

"Chase never did tell me what he wrote in that letter he gave to Cotton Turner. Did you read it?"

"No," I said. I unbuttoned my shirt and handed the newspapers to her.

She pushed them back at me. "Find the letter and read it to me," she said shyly.

The letter was on the editorial page.

" 'Editor: It has come to my attention that a local rancher has accused the residents of the Sweetwater Valley of committing various crimes and harboring criminals. If this be true, then I join the honorable Reese Clarke in calling for lawful prosecution. However, as a resident of the valley myself and as a longtime resident of Wyoming Territory, I can bear no witness relative to these alleged crimes. As a citizen, I, too, must request that an officer of the law come to the Sweetwater Valley for the purpose of learning the truth. Law and order must prevail. For one day settlers of all backgrounds will settle in the Sweetwater Valley, as they have settled throughout our western lands in years past. The future of the valley is golden indeed.

" 'Upon learning of the sale of the White and Rocking JD Ranches to Eastern speculators, I must voice my sorrow at the prospect of our territory being thrown into the hungry jaws of those who would have these precious lands become nothing more than open pastures for a few wealthy entrepreneurs who have never ventured west of the Hudson River to trade among themselves as so many cards in a child's game. Perhaps these speculators are the criminals Reese Clarke should address himself to.

Chase Malone, Sweetwater Valley.' "

Ella whistled softly. "I didn't know Chase could write that way. His letter sounded better than Reese Clarke's, didn't it?"

My eye was caught by a paragraph on the editorial page that began SWEET-WATER CONTROVERSY. I read it aloud. " 'In the current controversy that threatens to bring the waters of the Sweetwater River to a boil, your editor reminds all readers of the wisdom of seeking the truth rather than being swayed hour to hour or week to week by heated accusations that employ the wildest exaggerations. Name calling and dead fish have a common odor.' "

Ella laughed. "Wait until Chase reads that."

Chase Malone did read it late that afternoon. After the rain stopped I walked through the wet grass and up the muddy wagon ruts to the saloon. I gave him the papers and delivered Cotton Turner's message. Chase Malone laughed dryly and swore. He said he would get right to work on a reply. When I told him Ella had asked him down for supper, he nodded absently.

I walked back to the cabin, but instead of going inside, I went into the barn and let the horses out. They wandered through the yard and went out into the grass. The sunlight was out of the valley, but the late afternoon sky overhead was blue and spotted with broken gray clouds.

I looked up at the cliffs where the riders had been during the rain. If they were there now, I couldn't see them. I wondered if they were C Bar riders who wanted to go to the saloon, but were afraid to go against Reese Clarke's orders.

When Chase Malone walked into the yard, I shooed the horses back into the corral. I washed up and went into the cabin. Ella was frying chicken and had just taken fresh bread from the oven. Chase Malone asked me about my trip to town. After I told him, I mentioned that Sheriff Hobbs had been keeping an eye on me.

"That's his way," Chase Malone said. "He'll pass every day doing nothing but standing around Main Street, drawing his pay. Maybe I'll shake him up a little tomorrow."

Ella asked over her shoulder, "Are you going to town tomorrow, Chase?"

"I'm going to deliver a letter to Cotton Turner myself," he said. "What he told Boomer today is right. If I let that brand

261

accusation go unanswered, it will look mighty bad."

"What are you going to say?" I asked.

"I finished the letter just before I came down here," Chase Malone said. "I wrote the truth. I've done my damnedest to have a brand registered in this territory. First my papers were lost. It took me four months just to find that out. Then I got an unsigned letter from the Cattleman's Association stating there would be some delays. No whys or whens or anything. I applied again after the first of the year, but I haven't heard a thing. I know Reese Clarke is behind this. I can't prove it, but I know he's doing it. I reckon what I'll have to do this summer is take the train to Cheyenne and start a lawsuit. Isn't that a hell of a thing to go through just to have a brand registered?"

I was hoping Chase Malone would ask me to ride into town with him, but after supper he told me to go with Ella to White Wolf's camp in the morning. She might need some help, he said.

"You can spend the rest of the day hunting old One Eye and practicing your shooting," Chase Malone said. "Mark off a hundred paces and try hitting a can from there. You won't get much closer than that to One Eye. If you can hit a can from that far off, then you won't have any trouble dropping that steer."

Early that evening we heard a horse outside and then a familiar voice helloed the cabin.

"Buck," Ella said in surprise.

Ella opened the door. "Why, howdy, Buck. Come on in and set."

Buck Stone tramped in. Chase Malone welcomed him. Nodding at us, Buck took off his coat and sat at the table without saying a word. I saw something in his face, something that made him look hard.

"Well, I done quit," he said.

"Quit?" Ella exclaimed.

He nodded and pursed his lips together.

"What happened?" Chase Malone asked.

Buck shrugged. "Same old thing. One of those Texans came up with a short count in one of the herds. Clarke jumped me about it. I told him I never met a Texan who could count past ten. Clarke got madder and I got madder. So I drawed my time."

"What Texans are you talking about?" Chase Malone asked.

"You remember that young squirt who was in the saloon with us the other night? Well, he and his older brother hired on

263

about a month ago and things ain't been the same since. They're trying to run the C Bar behind my back and Clarke ain't done a thing to stop it. I believe he's egged them on, if anything. I believe that young Texan told Clarke about us going against his orders about being in your saloon. Hank and Bob and Smiley and me got fined five dollars. Bob quit on the spot. You know how hot he gets. I couldn't blame him. Hank's ready to quit if he can figure out a way to pay off his debts to Clarke."

"Did the young Texan get fined, too?" Chase Malone asked.

"So he claims," Buck said. "I don't know for sure. Anyhow, I believe he was the one who told."

Buck and Ella looked at each other for a long moment. Ella was silent, but her brow was knotted.

"What do you aim to do, Buck?" Chase Malone asked.

Buck breathed out loudly. "Well, I reckon I'll ride into town and see if I can find old Jake. Me and him can ride up north and maybe hire on with one of the big Montana spreads. That's where Bob went. He has relations up there and every time they wrote to him they bragged up on the country and told him how easy it would be to hire on. The way I look at it, if Jake's alone nobody will hire him. But if me and him go as partners, we won't have no trouble."

"That sounds like a good idea," Chase Malone said.

Ella's voice sounded hollow when she said, "Sure will be sorry to see you go, Buck."

"Goddammit, Ellie, I'm sorry to go. If I was like Chase here, I'd homestead in this valley. I know how happy you are here, Ellie. You're a lot happier out here than you were in town. I can see it in your face. I've thought about trying my hand at it. But I just can't do it. It ain't in me. I wish it was, but it ain't."

Ella nodded, but she didn't look at him. She stared at the table top. "I can understand that."

"Well," Buck growled, "then you understand more than I do. I wish I had it in me to stay."

"You don't need to rush off," Chase Malone said. "Why don't you stay around here for a few weeks? Do some fishing. I'll break out the good whiskey."

Buck smiled crookedly. "You ain't got no good whiskey, Malone." Then he said,

"Naw, I got the itch to ride the hell out of here. I want to get in to town tonight. I just stopped by here to say so long. I wanted to say something to the boy, too."

I looked across the table at Buck. He said, "I remember carrying on about the bad life of a cowboy and telling you not to follow that life. What I said was true enough, but I didn't have no call to be handing you a load of advice. A man has to follow his lights. If you aim to do some cowboying, then I'd hate to see any drunk cowboy like me talk you out of it. Good luck to you."

Buck Stone stood up, put his coat on, and shook hands all the way around. Chase Malone told him it wouldn't be the same around here without him. Ella nodded at him and whispered goodbye. Buck touched the brim of his Stetson in a formal way, and then left.

CHAPTER XVII

In the morning Ella and I found White Wolf sitting up inside his tepee. A buffalo robe was draped around his shoulders and another heavy, furry hide of some kind covered his lap.

As we had walked into the camp that morning, I saw the Indian girl tending a cook fire. When she saw me, she stood up and walked into the trees. Ella smiled at me and shrugged.

I ducked into the tepee after Ella and watched her change White Wolf's bandage. The day-old bandage was stained by a small patch of darkened blood. The old squaw sat against the far side of the tepee, watching Ella wrap the new bandage around White Wolf's chest. Ella tied it snug.

As Ella worked, White Wolf sat and watched me in stern silence. I smiled at him. He nodded once, but said nothing. Though he looked much stronger than I had expected, his face was slack and deeply lined as though he was very tired.

Behind White Wolf was his empty holster with a belt wrapped around it. I thought he probably knew by now that the Indian girl had thrown his revolver into the river. Beside the empty holster was a quiver of arrows and a bow.

Ella spoke to White Wolf in a low, comforting voice. She told him he had to stay quiet for several days because he had lost so much blood and because his wound needed time to close up and heal. White Wolf didn't answer or even nod at her. He kept looking at me in a stern way.

Ella stood up and said to me, "You know damn well he'll be up and running around as soon as he can get on his feet."

She had turned to leave and I stood up to follow when White Wolf spoke: "I have vision of the boy."

Ella looked down at him. "You won't be dreaming about anything if you don't stay quiet. Lay down now."

White Wolf ignored her. "Soon enemies come."

"Now, don't you scare the boy, White Wolf," Ella said.

White Wolf lay down and closed his eyes. The old squaw got up and pulled the robe over him and fussed with him until he growled at her. Then she sat down.

"Come on, Boomer," Ella said.

We walked out of the camp and through the cottonwood grove to the brush corral. I looked for the Indian girl, but didn't see her. Ella and I walked along the wagon ruts back to the cabin in silence.

I spent the rest of the morning working up stove wood and spading some more ground for Ella's garden. In the afternoon I saddled up the pony and hunted for One Eye. I rode into half a dozen draws in the cliffs, working my way up to the north fence.

It was the farthest I'd ever been up the valley. Unlike the narrowing south end of the Sweetwater Valley, the north opened up into flat grasslands, spotted with sagebrush. The cliffs fell away to a low ridge of red rocks. The trees along the river thinned out and were not as tall or as thick as in the valley.

I was curious about the course of the river and wanted to follow it. I wanted to explore it as the trappers must have felt the need to follow the river in the old days. I tried to imagine how it must have been in those days, before everything got mixed up with people settling the land. I looked at Chase Malone's north fence and tried to blot it out, but couldn't. Then I tried to imagine how the valley would be when it was settled up, as Chase Malone expected it to be. Though I looked forward to seeing his vision of the future come true, at the same time I wished I could be all alone in the Sweetwater Valley, with no fences and no threats from Reese Clarke.

I glanced at the low sun and knew I wouldn't have much time to follow the river. I decided to save it for another day. Instead I rode along the fence line. I found it to be in good condition. That meant One Eye was south of here. It was a long valley, but at least I had a starting place now. I rode back to the cliffs and entered a shaded draw. I surprised a few stray cattle. They were as wild as deer. They ran up the draw as far as they could, then milled around in fear. One Eye was not among them.

When I turned the pony and started to ride out, some markings along the flat edge of a red rock caught my eye. The markings were in black and were faded, but I could see that they showed several running animals drawn in a childish but graceful way. There were human figures behind the animals, running, too. Above them was a round symbol that reminded me of the sun symbol painted over the opening of

White Wolf's tepee.

I rode into a few more draws that afternoon but found no sign of One Eye. At that strange time of day when the sun was out of the valley, but the sky overhead was still sunlit, I went to the "firing range." I stepped off a hundred paces and fired a dozen rounds at a tin can. I didn't hit it once. Tired, I quit, wishing Chase Malone had been there to tell me what I was doing wrong.

But I didn't see Chase Malone until noon of the next day. Ella and I had just finished eating when he rode into the yard on his big skitterish horse. He came into the cabin carrying a branding iron.

"I had MacRae make this yesterday," he said, laying the branding iron on the table.

Ella held it up and read it: "EC connected?"

The letters were backward. Chase Malone said, "Ella and Chase, connected."

"Oh, Chase," Ella said.

"Now all I have to do," he said, "is go to Cheyenne and burn it into the door of the Cattleman's Association office. That ought to make it legal."

Ella laughed. "I'd like to see that."

"Well, why don't we start out with this door?" Chase Malone said. "Boomer,

271

while I'm getting a bite to eat, why don't you build a little fire out in the yard? We'll heat up this iron and try it out."

I built a fire, using coals from the cook stove for a starter, and put the branding iron in it. When Chase Malone was through eating, he and Ella came outside. He squatted before the fire, looking at the brand. Then he lifted it by the handle and turned it over. After waiting a while Chase Malone took it out of the fire. He handed it to Ella.

"Ella," he said in a deep voice, "brand that old log steer alongside the ass."

Ella laughed and pressed the hot iron into the cabin door. Smoke rolled off in a cloud until she pulled the iron back. The reversed letters left the right imprint: EC.

"Chase, that's the best brand in the territory," Ella said.

Chase Malone nodded. "I'll feel better about it when it's registered."

That afternoon Chase Malone and I rode to the firing range. I had told him what had happened the day before when I'd fired from a hundred paces.

"All you need is time to grow into that rifle, Boomer," he said. "When you're older and a little huskier, you'll be able to handle it better. Right now, I think you ought to use the sitting position for distance shooting."

Chase Malone sat on the ground and showed me how to prop my arms on my legs. When I fired from the sitting position, my first six shots were hits.

"That's good shooting!" Chase Malone said. "You've got a good eye, Boomer. Old One Eye's days are numbered."

It was easy for me to hold the rifle steady from the sitting position. Out of eighteen shots that afternoon, two missed. Chase Malone bragged on me and told me not to worry over the two misses because a steer was one hell of a lot bigger than a tin can.

"If you ever catch One Eye standing still," Chase Malone said, "he's as good as dead."

"But what if he's running?" I asked, remembering that the only time I'd seen him he was running at full speed.

"Then you'll have to do your best," Chase Malone said. "Oh, it won't be easy dropping that crazy steer. You've got the eye and the rifle that will do it. But just because he's loco doesn't mean he's stupid. I reckon he's been shot at by other ranchers. He's pretty wise by now."

That week flew by as though blown by a desert wind. I helped Chase Malone with the south fence and did chores for Ella. She had been right about White Wolf. As soon as he started feeling better, he was up and around. Chase Malone told Ella not to worry about him. He said as soon as White Wolf steals another horse or two, he'll be as good as new.

In the afternoons Chase Malone and I fired our rifles. I spent the early evenings hunting for One Eye. I never even got a glimpse of him. I wondered aloud to Chase Malone if he had left the valley.

"Not likely," Chase Malone said. "He's around somewhere. All of the shooting we've been doing might be making him wary of this area. We might quit for a couple of days and see if he shows." I saw him wink at Ella. "One Eye probably knows what a crack shot you've become. He's laying low to stay out of your way."

I said I doubted that. Chase Malone spent more time at the cabin that week than he had in all the time I'd been there. He and Ella seemed closer now. I wondered if it had anything to do with Buck Stone's leaving.

"I've ridden up plenty of those draws where One Eye might hide," I said, "but I haven't turned up anything but stray cattle and jackrabbits. Some of the draws open

274

out into the desert. It would be a steep climb, but I wonder if One Eye hides out in one that has a back door to it."

"That's a good way to put it, Boomer," Ella said, laughing. "You're starting to sound like a goddam Wyoming cowboy."

I felt embarrassed then, but embarrassed in a good way.

"You might be right, Boomer," Chase Malone said. "What you need to do is to look for a single set of tracks. Most of the strays that get back in those draws will be in small bunches. But old One Eye is a bunch quitter. He's a loner if there ever was one."

At the end of the following week Chase Malone rode to town and came back with several copies of the Sunbonnet *Global News.* Cotton Turner had written a series of editorials telling of the benefits of the Homestead Act and other land laws that permitted the settling of the West. One editorial was headlined NO FEUDAL EMPIRES IN AMERICA. Cotton Turner gave his readers several history lessons about the overthrow of some European governments. Possession of land by the common people was one of the founding principles of the United States, he wrote, and attempts to reverse this principle would lead to revolution.

The only reply to these editorials was from a rancher in the southern part of the county. He wrote that the ranchers of the high desert needed more acreage to support a given number of cattle than the ranchers who were located in the lower grasslands. The rancher ended his letter with a long quotation from Revelations. When Ella asked what he was getting at, Chase Malone said he wasn't sure.

But Reese Clarke had stopped writing letters to the Sunbonnet *Global News*. Chase Malone took this as a victory.

"Reese Clarke will have to scratch his head and try something else," he said.

Reese Clarke did try something else. I'd found a single set of tracks and had followed them into a draw near the north boundary of Chase Malone's claim. The tracks looked fresh and I rode into the draw with the Henry rifle at the ready.

But I found a cow who bawled miserably at being lost. I circled behind her and ran her out. When I came out of the draw, I was met by two C Bar riders. Both had yellow slickers tied behind their saddles and suddenly I knew these were the two men I'd seen in the rainstorm.

One was the young Texan who had been

in Chase Malone's saloon the night the riders had come after Buck Stone. The other was older, but he resembled the young one in his face and in dress. Both wore bright scarves and flashy shirts. Their shining boots had sharp pointed toes and colorful stitching like the pair I'd admired in Rodriguez's shop. The rowels on their spurs jingled with the slightest motion.

"Hand over that ol' rifle, sonny boy," the young one said.

I was slow to understand what he meant. "It's not mine. I can't loan it out."

The oldest one chuckled. I glanced at him, but a sudden blur of movement made me look back at the young one. A revolver was in his hand, the round, dark opening of the barrel pointed at my chest.

"Sonny boy, ya'll hand over that rifle or I'll blow a hole through you." I heard a soft click as he thumbed back the hammer.

The older one rode close to me and lifted the rifle from my hands. I heard my own voice shake when I asked, "What are you doing?"

"Save your questions for Mr. Clarke, sonny boy," the young one said. He motioned to the older one. "All you have to do now is follow him. Can ya'll handle that?" He sneered at me. I knew he was trying to act older than he was. But I saw something in him that was cold and mean, as though he would like to shoot someone.

I followed the older Texan toward the north end of the balked, then stepped gingerly over the downed wires. I heard the young one laugh, but I didn't look back at him.

We rode out of the north end of the valley where it opened up into flat grasslands. We crossed the river and passed the biggest herd of cattle I'd ever seen. Cowboys were working the herd. I guessed they were getting ready for spring roundup.

We rode straight out across the high desert and two hours later we dropped into a huge, grassy basin. We joined a ranch road that took us through a gate marked C BAR.

The main house was a two-story building set in the shade of cottonwoods. A long bunkhouse and blacksmith shop were off to one side. Beyond them I saw a patchwork barn and pole corral.

Reese Clarke came out of the main house as we rode into the yard. He stood on the front edge of the porch, hands on his hips, smiling at me. "Step down, young man. Come on inside."

He spoke to me like I was a guest he had

invited. I stepped out of the saddle and tied the pony at the rail. I took a step toward the older brother and reached up for my rifle. He pulled it back, but as he did, he looked at Reese Clarke. A signal must have passed between them for he handed the Henry down to me.

"Come on inside, young man," Reese Clarke said again, still using a friendly voice.

I went through the door of the house that he held open for me. In the front room was a big stone fireplace, flanked by leather-covered chairs. A bear rug stretched out on the floor before the hearth. On the mantel of the fireplace an old model Winchester was mounted on two pegs. I recognized the round stones that made up the chimney. They looked like the same ones Chase Malone and I had been digging out of fence post holes for the past two weeks.

"Lean that old rifle against the wall there, Boomer," Reese Clarke said. "That is your name, isn't it? It's a nickname, I suppose. Well, sit down there beside the bear. How about a cup of coffee? Wong?"

A Chinese cook poked his head out of a room that I took to be the kitchen, smiled and nodded at us. He wore a white apron and a white hat that looked like it was puffed up full of air. He must have had the coffee ready for he no more than turned around and came out with a tray holding two cups and a plate of sweet muffins.

I didn't touch the muffins or the coffee. Reese Clarke slapped his hands together and rubbed them. I thought he was expecting me to say something about his house. He looked around the room, then at me.

"That's quite a rifle you carry, Boomer. An old Henry, isn't it?"

"It's not mine," I said.

"Oh? Whose is it?"

"Chase Malone's."

A sour look crossed his face, but he caught himself and in the next moment he was smiling again. He sat in the chair across the bear rug from me.

"Boomer, you may not believe it, but I'm your friend. I sent for you because I want to have a talk with you. Will you hear me out?"

"That young Texan said he was going to shoot me," I said.

"He shouldn't have done that," Reese Clarke said, frowning. "I apologize for him."

"I want to go back to the valley," I said.

"Now, now," he said easily, "all I ask is

that you hear me out."

"You could have come to the valley and talked to me."

"I could have," Reese Clarke said, "but I wanted you to see the C Bar."

"Why?"

"I'll get to that, Boomer. But I want you to sit back and hear me out. Will you do that?"

I looked down at the bear hide. Its glass eyes looked wet. The sharp teeth in the opened mouth made the bear head look fierce and ready to leap up.

"Malone and that woman will soon be leaving the Sweetwater Valley, Boomer —"

"They aren't leaving," I said.

"Now, hear me out," Reese Clarke said. "You don't know all there is to know about this . . . business. Malone will be leaving the valley in a few days. I've been in contact with my lawyer who in turn has contacted the sheriff. Sheriff Hobbs will be coming to the Sweetwater Valley within the week. He'll serve eviction papers on Malone and that woman. They're squatters."

"No, they aren't!" I said.

"My lawyer tells me otherwise," Reese Clarke said with an easy shrug. "But that isn't the reason I sent for you. The real reason is of great importance." He paused,

281

watching me. "I've seen you on several occasions, Boomer. I've seen you more times than you know. I've asked around about you, but have discovered very little. You may wonder why I've gone to so much trouble."

He paused again. I thought he was waiting for me to say something. Then he went on. "As I once mentioned to you, I lost my only son a few years back. He was taken by an Injun sickness. So was my beloved wife. I haven't allowed an Injun on C Bar land since. But what I was saying was that I've liked what I've seen of you, Boomer. You're a fine lad. And I believe you'll be smart enough to accept a rather gracious offer.

"The offer is this: I'm prepared to hire you. You'll not only work on the C Bar, but you'll live here in the main house. I have a room fixed up for a boy of your age. I know you'll like that. I'm offering you that along with top wages — forty a month and found."

I felt him looking at me, but I couldn't meet his eyes. I kept looking at the bear's head. "I want to stay in the valley."

Reese Clarke said, "The Sweetwater Valley will soon be a part of the C Bar."

"How?"

He shrugged it away. "It's merely a legal matter." When I didn't say anything, he added, "You look like you don't believe me."

I didn't say anything.

"Take my word for it," he said. "It's true. Boomer, I'm offering you the run of one of the finest ranches in the territory. And I'm offering you much more than that, if you're sharp enough to see it."

I looked back at him. "I want to go back to the valley, Mr. Clarke."

He winced and came out of the chair like it was on fire. "The chance of a lifetime is in your lap! Can't you see it?"

Reese Clarke caught his breath and walked over to the fireplace. He turned back to me, saying, "I've learned that no one knows who you are or where you're from. That's uncommon in a boy your age. It means you're running from something — or someone. Am I right?"

I didn't answer.

"You won't even talk to me. Well, I'm telling you that you won't be able to stay in the Sweetwater Valley if you stay on with Malone. He's leaving. So's that woman. Now, where does that leave you, Boomer?"

"I'd go with them," I said. "But I don't think they're going anywhere."

"And what makes you think that?"

"Chase Malone was a lawyer before he came out here," I said. "If he was breaking the law, he'd know it."

"Why, sure, he knows it," Reese Clarke said. "But he doesn't think I know it. I'll make a believer out of him before the week's out. You can bank on that."

I felt hot and sweaty. There was something wrong about the whole thing, but I couldn't sort it out in my mind. All I knew was, I'd never be happy living in Reese Clarke's house.

"You understand the job I'm offering you, don't you?"

I nodded.

"And you're saying no to it?"

I nodded again.

"Can't you say it out loud?" There was almost a sneer in his voice, a taunt, that suddenly reminded me of the way my father often spoke to me when he wanted me to do a job I didn't want to do.

"No, Mr. Clarke," I said, meeting his eyes. "I can't take the job."

Reese Clarke turned away from me, scowling. "Buck never told me you were slowheaded. Get out."

CHAPTER XVIII

"Where the hell you been?" Ella asked when I rode into the yard that evening. Chase Malone came out of the cabin behind her, a worried look on his face.

I climbed off the pony and told them what happened, leaving out a few things. I told them the Texans had pulled down the north fence and I had gone to the C Bar Ranch with them, but I didn't say the two brothers had taken me away at gunpoint.

"Reese Clarke offered me a job on the C Bar," I said. "He told me you were going to have to leave the valley. He said the sheriff would come up here this week to serve eviction papers on you."

Chase Malone snorted. "He can't evict anybody from public lands, Boomer. Clarke's running a bluff."

I said, "He told me his lawyer was drawing up some papers of some kind and it was all legal."

Chase Malone shook his head. "Our claims are registered with the land office. Sounds to me like he's bribed the sheriff to

285

come up here to scare us off."

"Let him try," Ella said.

Ella put her arm around my shoulders. "You must be half starved, Boomer." She asked Chase Malone to take care of my pony as she walked me toward the cabin door. "You sure gave us a scare, I'll tell you. I thought a rattlesnake had got you. I was worried sick."

Behind us Chase Malone said, "I was worried, too, Boomer. I thought you'd run off with my rifle."

Ella laughed and asked me, "What did you say to Reese Clarke when he offered you a job?"

"I told him I already had one."

Ella tightened her grip on my shoulders. "Well, it's a good thing I kept your supper warm, then, isn't it?"

When Chase Malone walked into the cabin he said he didn't expect Sheriff Hobbs to come into the valley at all. Hobbs wasn't that much man. I wanted to believe Chase Malone, but I couldn't. He hadn't heard the way Reese Clarke talked. It hadn't sounded like a bluff to me.

"I'd like to find those young Texans," Chase Malone said. "Somebody needs to teach them how to use a gate."

Ella said, "Maybe we ought to ride over

to the C Bar come morning."

"I was thinking that, too, Ella," Chase Malone said. "But I've decided against it. We might be playing into Reese Clarke's hands by making a ruckus. Time is on our side. I believe we ought to sit tight."

During that week Chase Malone and I worked on the fences. He had started carrying his Winchester with him. Though nothing was said, I kept the Henry rifle with me, too.

It took most of a day to repair the damage done by the Texans. After that we went back to digging post holes and setting posts for the south fence. I kept watching for Sheriff Hobbs to come riding into the valley, but he never came. By the end of the week I had begun to think Chase Malone was right about Reese Clarke running a bluff.

And by the end of that week we were within spitting distance of the cliffs. Chase Malone said we would be able to string the wire in a day. If we took two days to set the last of the posts, then we were within three days of finishing the job.

I couldn't find the words to explain to Chase Malone what that meant to me. When we'd started the job, it had looked impossible to me. The red cliffs were a long ways off from the tree line. All I could think about was all the mistakes I'd probably be making and how Chase Malone would sooner or later get mad at me as my father always did when he had given me a job to do. But Chase Malone and I had worked side by side as two men would, and now, looking back along the line of fence posts that stretched all the way to the tree line, I was filled with a good feeling. Yet I didn't know how to explain it to Chase Malone.

As we drove the buckboard back to the cabin that afternoon, Chase Malone said, "I hate to string any wire until One Eye is out of our hair, Boomer. Between him and those two Texans we won't be able to keep a fence up from one day to the next."

"I found a single set of tracks like you said I should watch for," I said. "The tracks are near the cliffs. I've followed them into quite a few draws, but I haven't seen anything of One Eye yet."

"Well, maybe you're on to him," Chase Malone said. "Keep after those lone tracks."

When we got back to the cabin, I helped Chase Malone unhook Billy and Bobby from the buckboard. There was still plenty of daylight left, so I saddled the pony to go out after One Eye. The pony was ready for a ride. When I climbed into the saddle, he danced sideways across the yard.

"Can't you handle that Indian cayuse?" Chase Malone asked.

"He's picked up some bad habits from the worthless plug you ride," I said.

Ella had been standing in the doorway of the cabin, watching us. She must have been making bread, for she wiped white powder from her hands and arms with a white towel. "That's telling him, Boomer," she said.

Chase Malone turned toward her. He growled and scraped his feet on the ground like a bull. Then he made a run for the doorway. Ella shrieked. She threw the towel at him and backed into the cabin.

I didn't wait to see the battle. I turned the pony and rode out of the yard, cut south, and started out across the grassland. When I glanced back at the tree line, I saw White Wolf standing beside a cottonwood tree. The Indian girl stood near him.

I took off my Stetson and waved at them. White Wolf raised his hand to me. The Indian girl turned and walked back into the shadows of the trees.

I hunted One Eye until the sun was out of the valley. I picked up the lone set of tracks again and followed them into several draws. I scared up some strays, but never even got a glimpse of the locoed steer.

I rode back to the cabin and found supper burning on the stove. Smoke rolled out of the open doorway. I rushed inside, grabbed the smoking skillet, and set it on the ground outside.

No one was around. I stood in the yard, trying to think what had happened, when I noticed the towel laying on the ground where Ella had thrown it at Chase Malone. Then I saw that the corral was empty. Ella's buckboard was gone.

I mounted the pony and rode up the wagon ruts toward the saloon. I had gone only a short way when I saw a strange thing. Billy and Bobby, hooked up to the buckboard, were out in the high grass, grazing. My first thought was that Ella and Chase Malone must be out there, too.

But they weren't. No one was. It appeared the team had wandered out there by themselves. I rode around the wagon and cut an angle across the valley toward the saloon. Then I saw them. My heart went wild.

Ella and Chase Malone were hanged from a cottonwood tree beside the saloon. Three men were near the bodies. One rider was mounted, standing up in his stirrups, and the other two stood on the ground, looking up at the rider.

Their backs were to me. I rode as close as I dared and then slid out of the saddle. I waved my hand at the pony. He went down in the tall grass. As I took aim from the sitting position, I realized that two of the men were the Texans. The young one was standing up in his stirrups, going through Chase Malone's pockets.

The shot was a long one, all of a hundred yards, but the young Texan's broad back was a lot bigger than a coffee can. I felt the familiar jerk against my shoulder and heard the booming roar of the Henry rifle. I didn't wait to see if I'd hit him. I worked the lever and moved the sights to the second Texan. I steadied the bead in the V and lined the sights on his chest. He had turned to face me and had drawn his revolver. I heard his shouted curses and then some popping sounds followed by puffs of smoke. He seemed to be looking right at me when I squeezed the trigger.

I saw him thrown backward. His feet flew up. He skidded on the ground and then was still. The third man had mounted and spurred his horse around the back of the saloon. In a few seconds he came around the other side of the saloon at a run. I squeezed off a quick shot, but knew I'd missed even as I pulled the trigger. He rode up the valley and was soon out of sight. I'd recognized him. It was Sheriff Hobbs.

I waved the pony up on his feet and led him toward the saloon. Halfway there he balked at the sight and smell of death. I dropped the reins and walked ahead. The two Texans lay sprawled on the ground. My first shot had hit the young one at the base of the neck. Now his head was twisted at a strange angle, held to his body only by a torn piece of flesh. His open neck still oozed blood.

Ella's moccasins lay on the ground beneath her bare feet. Both Ella's and Chase Malone's faces were blue. Their heads were cocked to the side, the lynch ropes cutting deep into the darkened flesh. Chase Malone's dull eyes bulged out even more than they had in life. Ella's open mouth was filled with her tongue.

It all caught up with me then. I felt hot and weak, but I shook as though drenched in cold water. I dropped on one knee, bracing myself on the Henry rifle.

When my eyes cleared, I wiped a sleeve across my face and stood up. I saw the tracks of the buckboard leading out from under the cottonwood tree. Off to the side I looked at the prints of shod horses, but then I saw another set of tracks. They were made by a pair of iron-rimmed wheels and might as well have been a signature.

I caught the pony and followed the wheel tracks to the C Bar Ranch.

CHAPTER XIX

I turned the handle and kicked the door open. I stepped inside, bringing the barrel of the rifle level and making a sweep across the living room. No one was there.

I heard a foot scuff in the kitchen. Walking over the bear rug, I crossed the living room to the kitchen doorway.

"Come out," I said.

The Chinese cook poked his head around the door.

"Where is he?"

The cook stared at me. I brought the rifle to my shoulder. He swallowed hard and pointed at the staircase, then bobbed back behind the door. I took the stairs two at a time and entered a long hallway. I had opened the first door and found an empty bedroom when I heard Reese Clarke's raspy voice:

"In here."

The last door was half open. I kicked it open and brought the rifle barrel level. Reese Clarke sat on the edge of a bed clutching a framed photograph. He stared at me in a wild way. His shirt was open at the front and ripped as though he had tried to tear it off himself. A hunting knife lay on the floor at his feet.

"I knew you'd come."

"I'm going to kill you."

"I know," he said wildly. "I wanted to kill myself. I tried . . . even when I heard you coming, I tried . . ."

Suddenly I couldn't remember levering a fresh round into the chamber after shooting the second Texan. I worked the lever. A live round ejected. It clattered on the floor and rolled underneath a chest of drawers. On top of the chest I saw oval pictures of a young woman and a boy.

"Where's Hobbs?" I asked.

Reese Clarke looked away from me. "Been and gone."

"You paid him," I said.

"I paid him to draw up some papers to scare off Malone and El— the woman. I thought it would work until you told me Malone had been a lawyer once. But by then Hobbs and those two brothers had got together. They decided to do it."

"But you were there."

He nodded. "I was there."

"You could have stopped it!" My throat

was tight and I heard my voice rise high like a child's.

Reese Clarke looked at me without meeting my eyes and started to say something, but then he crumpled and began sobbing. The photograph fell from his hands to the floor. The glass shattered. I looked down at it and through the broken glass saw the nude picture of Ella with her foot up on a hassock that looked like a stuffed turtle.

I felt breathless and sick as though a wave of hot, foul water had washed over me. The room stunk of the man. I lowered the rifle and backed out through the door. I stood in the hallway for a moment and my last sight of Reese Clarke was of him curled on the bed, sobbing.

I was riding out of the ranch yard when I heard a familiar voice hail me. I reined up and turned back in the saddle. Hank walked toward me from the bunkhouse. He was shirtless and looked tired and dirty.

"What's going on?" he asked. "The sheriff rode out of here after having a hell of an argument with Clarke. I heard their yelling clean out to the bunkhouse. He no sooner rode out than here you come, riding hell for leather, carrying that big old rifle. What's going on?"

"Reese Clarke's a murderer," I said.

"What do you mean?"

I tried to tell him, but the words jammed up in my throat. I only said, "Help me bury them."

"Wait 'til I grab up a fresh horse," Hank said.

I rode out of the yard and through the C Bar gate. Hank caught up with me before I was out of the basin. It was early evening. The sky was pale. We rode across the high desert and into the valley in silence.

The two horses belonging to the Texans had wandered into the high grass in front of the saloon. They were grazing and trying to chew around their bits. My pony pulled up short of the hanging bodies. Hank reined up beside me.

"Don't this knot a man's gut," he said.

We cut down the bodies and buried them beside the saloon. I put Ella's moccasins back on her feet before we lowered her into the grave.

After we finished filling the graves and tamping down the earth, I helped Hank lift the bodies of the Texans and sling them over their saddles. Hank used their ropes to tie them on. I watched him run a loop around the young one's dangling head.

Though nothing was said, I knew he did it to keep the head from falling off.

Hank tied one horse to follow the other, then mounted and took the reins of the lead horse.

"I reckon I'll deliver these to Mr. Clarke," Hank said. "I never did figure out why he hired them. Neither one knew one end of a steer from the other. They never spent a night in the bunkhouse. Clarke put them up in the main house. None of us working hands could figure out what was going on. They looked like gunmen to me." He shook his head. "I don't blame Buck for quitting. I'll be quitting, too, now. I owe Clarke some money, but I reckon I'll have to find another way to pay him off. I can't stay after this."

Hank looked at the graves, then back at me. "What do you aim to do?"

"I don't know." I hadn't thought ahead until then. I looked down the valley. The light was fading. The air was still and smelled of spring.

"I have to go to town," I said.

Hank said, "Don't bet on making any trouble for Clarke. Folks won't go with that."

"I have to talk to Cotton Turner," I said.

Hank nodded. I mounted the pony.

Hank seemed ready to ride off, but something held him.

Then he said, "I plumb forgot your name."

"Boomer."

"I'll remember it," he said. "You're a tough son-of-a-bitch, ain't you? You ain't hard yet, but, by God, you're tough."

After we parted I rode back out to the buckboard. I tied the pony on behind and brought the wagon to the cabin. I had thought I would spend the night in the barn, but as I looked at the open-doored cabin, saw the white towel and skillet on the ground in front of the doorway, all the memories came back to me and I knew it was no use. I unhooked Billy and Bobby and shooed them out into the valley. Then I watered and lightly grained my pony, and left.

Night fell before I rode out of the valley, but as I crossed the river and passed through the break in the rocks that led to the open country, the moon came up over the cliffs behind me. I had no trouble following the old army road into town.

The moon was high when I rode down the empty main street of Sunbonnet. I passed the darkened hardware store, Skinner's Clothing, the newspaper office, and the Sunbonnet House. I turned the corner at the main intersection and crossed the railroad tracks. The only light I'd seen had been inside the train depot.

CHAPTER XX

Cotton Turner took the news hard, too. He sat at his desk in the newspaper office and scribbled notes from what I told him, shaking his head and muttering curses from time to time. The account I gave him was more complete than any I'd told anyone else.

"Well," he said when I'd finished talking, "you can bet Hobbs has put a lot of miles between him and Sunbonnet by now. Clarke paid him off so he won't be waiting around for a certificate of merit from the Cattleman's Association. And you can bet that Reese Clarke has calmed down and got his wits about him by now."

"What do you mean?" I asked.

"By now he'll be trying to think of ways to make himself look innocent," Cotton Turner said.

"But he was with the others!"

"Hold on," Cotton Turner said, "don't shout at me. I believe you. But you have to look at this as it would be seen in a court of law."

"I saw the tracks of his two-wheeled

buggy," I said. "I followed them to the C Bar. Reese Clarke told me he had been there. He was a part of it."

Cotton Turner nodded. "But in a court of law he would deny making the confession to you. In fact, he would very likely accuse you of assault. You entered his house with a gun. The cook will corroborate that. And Clarke would testify that he had no knowledge of tracks leading away from the scene of the lynching. You could prove nothing. Hank's testimony would be of little value."

"But Hank saw Hobbs at the C Bar," I said. "He heard Clarke and Hobbs arguing about the murders."

"He heard them arguing. Period. Reese Clarke could come up with an explanation for it. The court would have to accept it. As a matter of fact, with Hank's testimony and with the testimony Reese Clarke is likely to come up with, a hearing might only prove that you murdered the two Texans. Hank's testimony would work against you there."

"That isn't right," I said.

"I agree."

"What can we do?"

Cotton Turner pursed his lips. "I'm not sure at the moment. I want to give it some thought."

"No," I said. "Print that story as I gave it to you. It's the truth."

"It could easily turn out to be a jail sentence for you, Boomer," Cotton Turner said. "I won't do it. I want Clarke brought to justice as much as you do, Boomer, but printing that story isn't likely to do it."

My head pounded with anger. I was suddenly angered with everyone, even though I knew Cotton Turner was doing what he thought was best for me. But I knew, too, that Reese Clarke was a murderer.

"Where are you going?" Cotton Turner asked when I rose and turned to leave the newspaper office.

I didn't answer. I heard him say, "Come back at noon. I'll —" But then I was outside in the bright sunlight of early morning, mounting my whiteheaded pony, and trying to see into the future. For I knew one thing that was coming. I was going to kill Reese Clarke.

I rode out of town and back along the army road to the Sweetwater Valley. I was glad to be out of town and into the quiet open country. I had begun to realize that when people do a lot of talking, you can lose sight of the truth, of what is right.

I was back at the cabin by noon. Nothing had been touched. The frying pan and towel still lay before the open door of the cabin. This time I was able to look at them without feeling the painful tightness in my throat that meant tears were coming.

I built a fire in the stove. While the frying pan was heating, I went outside and found some eggs. I made a lunch of bacon and scrambled eggs and bread. As I broke off a hunk of the bread, I realized that Ella must have just taken it from the oven yesterday when the men came.

After lunch I went out to the barn. I packed up my gear. Then I saw Ella's gardening trowel hanging from a nail. I took the trowel back to the cabin, moved the kindling box, and dug into the packed mixture of dirt and ashes beside the stove. I pulled the money box out of the hole and set it on the table. I had filled the hole and moved the kindling box back against the stove when I noticed that it had become darker inside the cabin as though the sun had gone under a cloud. But I must have heard or felt something because suddenly I knew I was not alone. I whirled and faced the door.

"Now, I wonder what's in that little box." Sheriff Hobbs's squat figure filled the doorway. His revolver was pointed at my chest.

Hobbs grinned. "I figured that woman had a cache. Everybody said she left Coralee's with a trunk full of money." He jerked his head at the Henry rifle that leaned against the far log wall. "I reckon you're the joker who dropped them two Texans. I couldn't figure out who it was for the longest time. Then it came to me last night. Some piece of shooting, that was. I felt that last one buzz past my ear. Now, that was one long shot. I thought, That must be Malone's Henry doing that. Well, sure enough. But I come back, didn't I? I got me a brand-new Winchester out of the deal — and some old tin box you dug out of the floor. Open it."

I shook my head.

"Open it or I'll open you."

My whole body rocked with fear. For I knew he would kill me. The revolver was steady in his hand and I saw an odd look in his face.

"Ella had it," I said.

"Huh?"

"Ella had the key," I said. "She kept it around her neck."

Hobbs smiled, showing dark teeth. "That means you'll have to dig her up, don't it?"

"No!"

Hobbs laughed. "That notion don't appeal to you? Well, now maybe I can shoot that little lock off. It don't look too stout. Trouble is, I don't know which to shoot first — the box or you."

My mouth went dry and my heart tightened. Hobbs waved the revolver between my chest and the tin box in a teasing way. Then he laughed and pulled the trigger. The explosion seemed to rock the whole cabin. The box spun off the table and fell to the dirt floor, spilling bills and coins.

Hobbs's face was lit by surprise and pleasure, but then his eyes opened too wide and his mouth was stretched with pain. The revolver fell from his hand. He cried out, falling forward into the cabin. An arrow was buried in the middle of his back.

The screaming blur of flesh and buckskin that jumped upon the body turned out to be the Indian girl. She sat on Hobbs's body as though to hold it down, waving her knife overhead, screaming. I heard a low but sharp guttural voice outside. The girl stopped. She looked up at me and smiled.

When the girl began cutting Hobbs's skin at the back of his head, I quickly crossed the room to the doorway and stepped past her. Outside, White Wolf stood in the yard, holding the bow. A quiver of arrows was slung over his back.

I walked out into the yard and thanked White Wolf. He only nodded in reply, holding up three fingers. Then he motioned past me at the Indian girl. I turned and saw her coming, replacing the knife in the sheath at her waist. In her free hand she carried the stained arrow and Hobbs's bloody scalp.

As the Indian girl walked past me, she grinned and slapped me on the shoulder. She walked on, heading for the cotton-wood grove.

"No more kill," White Wolf said to me. He smiled and nodded, then turned away and followed the girl into the trees.

I went back to the cabin and dragged Hobbs's body inside. I gathered up the money that was strewn across the floor. Coins had rolled back under the bunk and up against Ella's cowhide trunk. I stuffed the money into my trouser pockets. I didn't take time to count it, but I thought it must be near two thousand dollars, give or take a few hundred. Anyway, it was more money than I'd ever seen in one place.

I emptied all the lanterns, pouring fuel

over the pine table and over Hobbs's body. After making a trail of fuel out the door and taking one last look around the cabin, I lit the fuel. The flame leaped into the cabin and made a *whump* sound as it hit the soaked table and clothing of the body. Soon flames licked at the logs.

I caught Hobbs's horse and stripped him. I gave him a slap and he ran out into the valley. I took the scabbard with Chase Malone's Winchester from Hobbs's saddle and put it on my own. Then I carried his saddle and bridle into the barn.

I had tried to think it out like Cotton Turner would have. If Hobbs's body had been found scalped, a man-hunt might have been started for White Wolf since it was known he often camped in the Sweetwater Valley.

But now only a charred skeleton would be found. It was a small favor I could do for White Wolf. He had done more for me than I could ever repay.

I mounted the pony and rode out to the wagon ruts. Chase Malone's Winchester was in the scabbard under my leg and I carried the Henry crossways as he had taught me. When I looked back and watched the fire take the cabin, I felt tired and older than I'd ever felt.

I didn't know when exactly, but sometime in the last hour I had realized that I would never be able to kill Reese Clarke. There had been enough killing. The deaths of five people were on Reese Clarke's shoulders. I knew if I took it on myself to kill him, it would only make me into the kind of man he was.

I was brought out of my thoughts when the pony suddenly shied. I thought the fire was bothering him, but then I heard a rumbling sound. I looked out across the grassland toward the cliffs and saw a roan shape coming at me. It was One Eye. Maybe the fire had stirred him up. As before, One Eye charged at a full run, then veered off and ran up the valley.

I didn't try for a shot. Let him run, I thought, turning the pony to follow the wagon ruts out of the Sweetwater Valley.

It was late evening when I got back to town. I left the pony at MacRae's livery. MacRae wasn't there, but a towheaded livery boy was. I told him what the pony needed and paid in advance. The livery boy was excited about seeing a real Indian war pony. He was about my age, but he acted like a kid.

I walked to the train depot and found out there was to be a midnight train. I bought a ticket and made arrangements to have the pony shipped East on the same train.

I crossed the tracks and walked along Saloon Row. I had an idea about going to Coralee's, though I wasn't sure why. All I had to tell her was about the death of Hobbs.

As I passed by the Shoofly, I took a long glance inside, hoping to see Buck and knowing I wouldn't. I saw Hank standing at the bar. I went inside.

"Why, howdy, Boomer," he said, when he noticed me.

I leaned against the high bar and put my foot on the rail as I had seen other men do. "Did you quit the C Bar?"

Hank nodded, "Yeah, I quit. Old Clarke's having a tough time of it. A few of the other boys quit after I told them what had happened on the Sweetwater. Clarke won't come out of his house. He won't hardly talk to nobody. Makes you feel sorry for him, don't it." He laughed dryly.

"Where are you headed?" I asked.

"North," Hank said. "I'm of a mind to hunt up Buck and Jake. Whatever outfit Buck's ramrodding is likely to be tolerable. The C Bar was a good outfit until Clarke got a-scared."

"Scared of what?" I asked.

"He knowed he was losing out to those speculators who bought up the White Ranch and the Rocking JD. He knowed they would be so strong they could take over the Sweetwater Valley if they was of a mind to do it. Before, when the ranches was smaller, the owners wanted to get along with one another. But things is changed. Clarke figured he was going to be left high and dry."

"Will he?"

Hank shook his head. "I don't believe so. The first bad winter we get is going to bury those speculators. They're so under-manned they won't be able to move their stock when they have to. Of course, they don't know that yet. But they'll learn. I give them two, three years. By then they'll want to sell out cheap."

"Have you heard from Buck?" I asked.

"Nope," Hank said.

"I thought you said he was a ranch foreman."

"I did," Hank said. "Nobody's told me, but I know he's ramrodding a ranch up there in Montana."

"How do you know?"

Hank glanced at me, then took a drink. "He was born one."

"How will you find him?"

"I'll ask around. Buck ain't hard to find. He has a way of getting his name knowed to folks. One day I'll find him. He'll be out on the range. I'll ride up to him and say, 'Howdy, Buck.' And he'll say, 'Why, howdy, Hank. You working for me again?' And I'll say, 'Yup.' And Buck'll say, 'Well, what're you sitting around here for? Get out there and work the moss off your butt.' "

I laughed harder than I'd laughed in a long time.

Then Hank said, "Why don't you grab up that little Injun pony and ride along with me, Boomer?"

I had to turn him down.

Hank didn't question me. "You know what you have to do," he said. "Maybe our trails will cross again someday."

"I hope so," I said.

Hank offered to buy me a beer, but I heard a train whistle. I said goodbye to him and walked back up to the depot. The train was due in at ten o'clock and due to leave at midnight. I wanted to be there in plenty of time so I could load the pony myself. I didn't know how he would load, and I didn't want a bunch of strangers beating him half to death to get him on.

I had walked down to MacRae's, got my pony and gear, and was leading him up the street when I saw a light in the newspaper office. I crossed the street and tied the pony at the rail.

Cotton Turner was inside, setting type. I tapped on the window. The editor turned and smiled when he recognized me.

"I'm damned glad to see you, Boomer," Cotton Turner said, opening the door. "You know, when you left here this morning, I had a bad feeling you were on your way to killing Reese Clarke."

Our eyes met. I said, "How do you know I didn't?"

"Because Reese Clarke rode into town this afternoon," Cotton Turner said "He got together with Judge Lindsay and the mayor and confessed his part in the lynchings."

"He did?"

Cotton Turner nodded. "The mayor told me he'd never seen a man look so bad. Clarke looked like he hadn't eaten or slept in a month. He told the judge that he couldn't live with himself any longer."

"Will there be a trial?" I asked.

"That's up to Judge Lindsay. Frankly, I doubt it. Clarke admitted being present at the lynchings, but it was the Texans and

Hobbs who actually did it."

"But Reese Clarke could have stopped it," I said.

"And that's what he has to live with, Boomer," Cotton Turner said. "The crime is a matter of public record now. I'm going to print your story. I'm setting it up now. After folks around here read your story and hear about Clarke's confession, I believe they'll have to take stock of themselves."

Cotton Turner looked out into the darkness of the street. He said, "I'm surely going to miss Chase Malone. I never met a man like him before. I never expect to again. He was something. I didn't know Ella except to say hello to her. But I remember something she said to me when I happened to see her in the land office. She was filing her claim on the Sweetwater that day. I wished her luck, and then I asked her why she was doing it. At the time I suspected it was only a scheme of Chase's to get another quarter section along the river. But Ella said to me, 'Mr. Turner, I'm going up there to settle.' That was all she said, but there was something in her voice when she said it that told me what it meant to her, how important it was to her. Do you understand what I mean?"

"Yes," I said.

Cotton Turner looked me over and said, "I'd tell you to come by tomorrow and get a free copy of the paper, Boomer, but I believe that's a train ticket I see sticking out of your shirt pocket. Is that midnight train yours?"

I nodded.

"That's an eastbound train. Are you going home?"

"Yes."

"Well, I hate to see you go. If you want, you can leave me your address and I'll send you a copy of tomorrow's paper in the mail."

I smiled at the bearded editor and held my hand out to shake. I was on my way home to face up to my father and to give his money back to him. And I wanted to give Boomer back his name, too.

"I wish you'd hold a copy for me," I said, gripping Cotton Turner's hand. "I'm coming back."

Stephen Overholser was born in Bend, Oregon, the middle son of Western author, Wayne D. Overholser. Convinced, in his words, that "there was more to learn outside of school than inside," he left Colorado State College in his senior year. He was drafted and served in the U.S. Army in Vietnam. Following his discharge, he launched his career as a writer, publishing three short stories in *Zane Grey Western Magazine*. On a research visit to the University of Wyoming at Laramie, he came across an account of a shocking incident that preceded the Johnson County War in Wyoming in 1892. It was this incident that became the inspiration for his first novel, *A Hanging in Sweetwater* (1974), that received the Spur Award from the Western Writers of America. *Molly and the Confidence Man* (1975) followed, the first in a series of books about Molly Owens, a clever, resourceful, and tough undercover operative working for a fictional detective agency in the Old West. Among the most notable of Stephen Overholser's later titles are *Search for the Fox* (1976) and *Track of a Killer* (1982). Stephen Overholser's latest novel is *Dark Embers at Dawn*.